A Messy, Beautiful Life

A Messy, Beautiful Life

SARA JADE ALAN

Entangled Publishing, LLC
2614 South Timberline Road
Suite 109
Fort Collins, CO 80525
Visit our website at www.entangledpublishing.com.

Entangled Teen is an imprint of Entangled Publishing, LLC.

Edited by Candace Havens
Cover design by Sam Heyn
Cover art by Sam Heyn

Manufactured in the United States of America

First Edition October 2017

In memory of Tyler Rebecca Byrd Smith

To my mom Evelyn, dad Don, and sister Theresa, for believing

To Brian and Emerson, for holding my heart

Chapter One

I could practically smell the nervous sweat under my pits as I peeked out from behind the curtains at the packed house. Porter Township High School had a brand-new theater where we'd been invited to perform tonight in the Comedy Mash-Up. It was a gorgeous space with a shiny wood stage and rows of red velvet seats that were currently filled with the butts of one hundred and eighty high school students.

Maneuvering from center stage through the darkness of the wings to the backstage area, I took a seat on the ratty couch that must have hosted at least seven generations of drama geek tears and farts. It was comforting to know that even if Porter's improv group, Scared Scriptless, had a theater that was newer and shinier than ours, it still featured the obligatory disgusting backstage area. I carefully set down the reusable water bottle with our team's mascot swimming around in it.

"Aye, Captain Ellie!" Quinn shouted in her best pirate voice as she ran through the backstage. She jumped into the seat next to me, releasing an explosion of cushion-fluff. "This is so exciting. Did you see how many people are in the audien—you…you brought Harold?" She pointed to the goldfish.

Spontaneous Combustion had named our group's mascot Harold after the most well-known improvisational form, the "Harold," created by Del Close from the iO Theater in Chicago. Since our school was in a suburb just outside of Chicago, we took pride in the fact we were born near some of the most famous improv theaters in the country—iO, Second City, the Annoyance Theater. Harold was our shout-out to that. As co-captain, it was now my job to take care of him, and in the first two weeks of school, I'd come to the conclusion that goldfish were highly underrated pets.

"Yeah, for our first show of the year, I made up a new policy that we'll bring Harold wherever we perform. For good luck. Right, lil' guy?" I pressed my finger to the side of the bottle, and he swam up, his tiny mouth making happy bubbles.

"What does your co-captain think of that?" Quinn raised her eyebrows, her eyes reminding me more than ever of a slow loris—those weird monkey creatures whose eyeballs take up a disproportionate amount of their face—but in a hazel, pretty-girl kind of way.

"Think of what? Endangering the life of goldfish?" Hana, the other co-captain, asked in her staccato way as she cracked open a can of fizzy tangerine juice and shrugged. "I'm cool with it."

"I just know you two will be great as our new captains." Quinn squealed and pulled me in for a hug. She waved Hana in, but Hana, not a hugger, chugged some of her drink and then belched at Quinn in defense.

I laughed. I loved Hana. She'd moved to Northglenn the summer before high school, but after being the only two freshmen cast in Spontaneous Combustion, it felt like we'd known each other our whole lives. I'd finally found a friend I could totally relate to. It didn't hurt that we lived on the same side of town—the ugly-apartment-complexes side, me in Glenshire Cove, and Hana in The Regency. "Such glamorous names for such humble little hovels," Hana loved to say.

"Ew," Quinn said as she released me from her love/death-grip.

With sweet Harold safe, providing us his goldfish good luck from his spot in the wings, we joined the other five members of our group onstage to get ready for the show.

As Hana and Quinn took their turns peeking out through the curtains, Quinn asked, "How did Scared Scriptless manage to get such a big turn out?"

"For starters, I imagine they don't use our group's zero-advertising marketing strategy," I said.

"Mmm." Hana was rubbing her cheek on the plush curtain, her eyes closed. "I want to steal this theater and put it in my bedroom so I can wake up on these golden floorboards snuggled in these velvety curtains every morning. Can I do that?"

"I believe in you." I smiled and clapped my hands together once. "Okay, we're about to start, let's get the group circled up."

"We're ready for this." Hana released the curtain and turned to us, looking more like a warrior than an improviser. "This place is awesome. We're gonna wreck some faces tonight." She gave Quinn a chest bump and then graced me with one.

"Ow," Quinn and I said in unison.

Hana Yoon: a Chihuahua who thought she was a pit bull. She had all the makings of an all-star athlete, minus the small details of her pint-size body and zero athletic ability. Amping up before performances was how she unleashed her competitive spirit, even if our improv show wasn't technically a competition.

The lights in the theater dimmed as the music swelled.

Over the music, a guy in the sound booth announced our group. "Welcome to Porter Township High School's Friday night Comedy Mash-Up! Pleeease put your hands together and welcome our guests for the evening, Northglenn High's SPONTANEOUUUUUUS COMBUSTION!"

As the red curtains parted, I could practically feel our collective stomachs flip.

Hana gave our group's standard spiel. "Tonight, we'll be doing a short-form style of improv similar to the TV show 'Whose Line Is It Anyway?' We'll get suggestions from you in the audience and create instant scenes based on your suggestions. Are you ready?"

The audience cheered, and we launched into our first scene. Our show clicked along as we played our favorite games of Arms Expert, Broadway Musical, and Replay. Hana and I traded off between emceeing, playing, and guiding our team from the wings.

Toward the end of our thirty-minute set, we started our last game and invited Scared Scriptless to play with us. In the game of Freeze, two players do a scene until someone on the sidelines yells "Freeze," then the players have to hold whatever pose they were in. Another actor tags one person out, takes on the same position but starts an entirely new scene that justifies that starting position. It continues as people call out "Freeze" and start new scene after new scene.

At one point, I was onstage with Chris, a massive guy who used to be on the football team. He was carrying me around completely tipped on my side as he shouted about finding "the lost statue," when someone from Scared Scriptless yelled, "Freeze!"

A boy from the other team ran up to tag one of us out, which meant I would soon either have to hold a stranger or be held by a stranger. *Fantastic.* The Porter boy was thin, but through his navy-blue T-shirt that read SCARED SCRIPTLESS in a bold font, his chest and shoulders had a nice amount of oomph. Before I got a good look at his face, he disappeared behind me.

He tagged Chris out. They exchanged spots, while I tried to hold my statue position on my side with one hand on my hip and one hand under my head, elbows out. Chris's large forearm left my waist and was replaced by a tan, leaner version. This wrist sported one of those wristbands for a cause, which nestled up to… Well, I'd have to describe it as the sexiest watch I'd ever seen—which was odd, since I'd never considered them sexy before. In fact, I was pretty sure I never used the word "sexy" to describe anything, except while being sarcastic (like when Hana jokingly made-out with her pudding cup at lunch and had brown goop all around her mouth I said, "Real sexy, Hana.").

As the boys continued to shift my weight for the pass, I let myself dwell on Porter Boy's watch—the thickness of the black leather band, the shininess of the silver face. The word "manly" came to mind. His thumb ever-so slightly grazed the bottom of my left breast as he took complete hold of me. Fortunately, I didn't have time to worry about it because he had started the scene.

Even though Porter Boy had proven he was confident physically carrying me, his character pretended to be awkward and shifted me back and forth while stuttering and umming.

The experienced improviser in me pushed past the inner freak-out all his touching was causing and reacted to his offer. I wiggled out of his clutches, and we faced each other, our eyes connecting for a second. His were a pleasing shade of brown—earthy but bright. When our gaze broke, the coolest thing happened. We both started doing the same thing at the same time: brushing each other off and saying things like, "ooh, sorry," and "err, excuse me…" We entered into some abstract game with each other.

Turning him around so his back was to me, I tapped him between his shoulder blades. As if reading my mind, he immediately fell back into my arms. I didn't know *why* I needed him to do that, or how he knew to do it, only that is was supposed to happen next in our weird game. I easily caught him and dragged him backwards. Our characters were in some alternate universe where they had to get somewhere but only one person could do the transporting at a time.

Sure, it made no sense whatsoever, but that was the glory of improv, and the audience loved it. Despite the bizarreness, Porter Boy and I were so committed that every new position — me getting a piggyback ride, him on my back like I was a horse — caused the audience to laugh harder.

Porter Boy pretended to come upon a stream. He mimed testing the water and then lay down in the imaginary stream and patted his chest, signaling me to climb on top of him. I gathered I was supposed to lie on top of him like he was a raft, so that's what I did. Putting my hands on either side of his shoulders, I lowered myself down like I was doing a slow push up. His breath. So much heat. The swish-rush-thump of his blood through his heart.

Then reality hit.

From the outside, it must have looked like a weird improv girl about to lie right on top of a strange boy. Onstage. In front of almost two hundred people.

We had been doing near-acrobatics for the past two minutes. Snippets popped into my mind — entangled arms, wrapped legs, arched backs. My brain processed the building energy of the audience, the rising laughter, the hoots and whistles, and I realized our scene must have looked like an epic dry-humping session.

Mortification enveloped me, like all the naked, peeing nightmares of childhood but without the happy escape of waking. I feared this might be one of those shuddery life-moments to etch a forever-home on my memory's instant-cringe list.

And yet. The rare connection, the out-of-body-ness... I understood what it felt like to be in the moment. I also knew there was "in the moment," focused but aware, and really *in* the moment, where everything outside the scene slipped away. It was what I'd read about in all our improv books—like some Holy Grail of improvisation. But I hadn't known it was possible to totally "lose your mind" and be *completely* in the moment. Now I did, and it was *fun*.

If only it could have happened in private.

But it hadn't. And we were still in it—I was hovering perilously close to his face, as all this flashback processed in the embarrassment quadrant of my brain in an instant. I made the mistake of looking him in the eyes.

Our faces were so close. His lips formed a shy grin on one side, revealing a single, irresistible, dimple. We cracked up, and I released the rest of my weight onto him in a fit of nervous laughter, my head falling in the crook between his neck and shoulder. My nose informed me I had a new favorite smell. As he brushed off some of my hair that had fallen in his face, his arm mashed against me in a nice and only slightly suffocating kind of way, and he shouted, "Will someone please yell freeze already?"

Someone from the audience yelled, "No! We're waiting for you to *do it*."

"Yeah!" the whole audience agreed in unison.

And then they chanted, "Do it! Do it! Do it!"

Oh my God. It hit me that I was, in fact, *still* laying on top of him. Super speedily I stopped sniffing him like some crazed wildebeest and jumped up, only to be left standing downstage, caught and bewildered, a flush of embarrassment crying out like a face tattoo.

I decided I really should quit improv.

It would make life so much easier.

Finally, Quinn rescued me by yelling, "Freeze!" and tapping Porter Boy out. Spontaneous Combustion had been asking for the guest improvisers' names, so as Quinn came to tag-out Porter Boy, she did the same.

"Everyone, please give Jason a big round of applause." And with that, Jason waved sheepishly and ran down the stage steps to sit back with the rest of Scared Scriptless.

My scene with Porter Boy—Jason—was all I could think about during my next scene with Quinn. People were laughing, but I was going through the motions, still reeling inside. Fortunately, I was saved from trying to get through another scene when Hana said, "And freeze! Thank you. That's our show." She let the audience clap a bit, then Spontaneous Combustion took our bows, and she shouted, "We'd like to thank Scared Scriptless for inviting us to play here tonight. Now, please give a big welcome to Porter's own: Scared Scriptless!"

Spontaneous Combustion took our seats in the front row of the theater as Scared Scriptless took the stage. My heart seemed to beat louder than the music that started up again.

A tall guy with curly hair and glasses who introduced himself as Owen addressed the audience. "Thanks, Spontaneous Combustion. Before we start our set, Scared Scriptless has an exciting announcement." Owen got mock-serious and made his voice low, rumbling into the microphone he was holding. "We were recently approached by some people who are a pretty big deal." He popped his words into the mic. "These comedy VIPs want to hold a contest right here." He pointed to the wood floor. "I'm talking about none other than your *favorite* online source for comedy. That's right—drum roll please…"

From the side of the stage, all the members of Scared Scriptless made drum roll sounds with their mouths or with their hands hitting against their thighs.

"This is big. Are you ready?" The audience cheered. Owen held the microphone a few inches from his face as he yelled, "Comedy Hub! Did you hear me? *Comedy Hub*. Here at Porter Township High School, Comedy Hub will be hosting a huge Comedy Contest for college-bound seniors from all over the Chicagoland area. The competition is only six weeks from today, on October thirteenth. Yes, it will be on Friday the thirteenth, but don't fear. It'll be *someone's* lucky day." Owen's pale skin turned splotchy red with the force of his screaming and excitement as his lanky limbs gesticulated wildly.

"The main part of the competition is a *standup* competition where the grand-prize winner will receive five hundred dollars. The winner will also…" Owen inhaled deeply, then raised his free hand above his head as he shouted, "have his or her set featured on Comedy Hub dot com." The audience became even crazier. I was really glad he chose to save this announcement until after our set.

I stole as many looks at Jason during Owen's speech as I could. He had a habit of running his hand through his hair to keep it out of his eyes. *Lucky hand.*

Owen continued pacing around the stage like a panther, unable to contain his enthusiasm. "There's even more. In addition to the standup competition, there will also be a sketch category, with each member of the winning sketch team—another drum roll is needed, guys…" Scared Scriptless provided another, louder drum roll sound effect for Owen. "One hundred dollars each for up to five members. Can you believe it?" He wiped his now-sweaty forehead while the audience continued to cheer. "The details were just posted to Scared Scriptless's website. Okay,"—all through the audience phones lit up—"back to your previously scheduled show. Scared Scriptless will now do a different style of improv from what you just saw. We do a long-form called the Harold and we need one suggestion to get us started."

Hana leaned over to me. "Ooh, here's your chance to try standup like you've always wanted."

"What are you talking about? I've never written a joke in my life."

"But you could. I've seen the way you watch it—like you're studying."

I shook off the idea. "I don't have anything interesting to write about. And even if I did, I'd be up against people who've probably, you know, done it before."

"Since when has standup been about something interesting? Usually it's about nothing."

"Okay fine, you do it then."

"Solo at the mic is not my style. And, I've got to focus on rustling up some assistant directing or producing opportunities before the ol' college apps are due. Can't prove to anyone I'm supposed to be in charge if I'm not in charge of anything," Hana said.

I scoffed. But I didn't tell her how hypocritical she was, because I was still reeling from the sensation of having left my skin onstage in my scene with Jason. Plus, now was my chance to focus on their show and stare freely at Jason for as long as I pleased.

By the end of Scared Scriptless's set, they managed to get all three storylines of their Harold to converge. Compared to our show, theirs was magic. And Jason was definitely one of the strongest improvisers in their group. His performance came off as effortlessly funny, and he had an incredible range of characters. What impressed me the most was that he was like a comedy surgeon, knowing exactly when to enter or exit a scene, or add the smallest detail to support his teammates and make the scene that much tighter.

I leaned over to Hana and Quinn and whispered, "Can we please get out of here as fast as improviserably possible?"

As I got up to join in the clapping, I caught Jason's eyes. He seemed to be staring right at me.

Yeah, I should definitely quit improv.

After the show, I grabbed Harold and tried to round up all the freshmen and sophomores in our carpool and get all eight members of our team to a centralized spot. While I had my guard down, the captain of Scared Scriptless—Mark Weiss, who was the son of Channel Seven News's affable weatherman—came up to invite us to an after-party.

"We're headed to J.C.'s house. You should come." He said this, theoretically, to all of us, but his eyes were in a laser-pointed lockdown on Quinn.

I didn't answer, too busy noticing the intensity of Mark's stare and how much he resembled his dad—they even had that same oddly tan skin.

Fortunately, Hana hadn't zoned out and could still form sentences. "We'd love to, but we've got a few young newbies with annoying curfews mucking up our hangout options."

"Damn. The good news is there will be a bigger party tomorrow night. You should all definitely come to that one. Yo, J.C." Mark, finally breaking his creepo gaze away from Quinn, shouted at his teammate and waved him over.

When I stopped trying to figure out if Mark's skin color was real or sprayed-on, I was surprised at who was jogging toward us. Somehow I'd managed to convince myself I wouldn't have to see him again until I'd better prepared myself. And yet, there he was, standing right next to me.

"Hey, nice show," he said to me.

"I thought your name was Jason," I blurted like a champ. Mark and Jason looked at me quizzically, and even Hana and Quinn cringed a bit.

"It is. Jason Cooper. First and last names. Mark has a thing about calling people by their initials." Jason did that one-corner-of-his-mouth smile again, as his brown eyes seemed to twinkle.

Could eyes really twinkle? That wasn't fair. Maybe it was his long lashes reflecting the stage lights and causing some illusion? I willed his eyes to stop looking so good. "Cool." A nervous, gulping, laughter-like sound lurched out of me. Apparently my wits had been taken hostage and beaten to death by my hormones.

Also, it was more evidence I hadn't had a lot of boyfriends. No serious ones at least. It wasn't that I was a total prude, but people are brave in different ways. Making a fool out of myself in front of hundreds of people by pretending to be someone else was way easier than in front of one person as the real me.

Hana, who had closed her eyes in pain, was taking a deep breath, trying not to laugh. *Thanks, Hana. Stay strong for me.* After a silent beat, she finally opened her eyes and came to my rescue. "Hello, Jason, nice to meetcha. I'm Hana, this is Quinn and Ellie. So. Mark tells us you're having a party Saturday and we're invited?"

Chapter Two

I sat on the kitchen counter eating Oatmeal Squares and kicking my heels against the ugly oak cabinets. The cabbagey smell of kimchi wafted over from our neighbor's apartment as images of last night's show and my tour de force of social ineptitude pinballed around my brain. Mom shuffled into the kitchen in her faded pajama set, a big toe poking through a slipper, reading glasses askew, her laptop in hand. She brightened when she saw me.

"How was your night with Aunt Heather?" I took a bite of my cereal.

"She forced me to join this stupid online dating service. Look at this."

Mom set the laptop on the counter, straightened her glasses, and clicked on her profile. "Now I have to write some BS about myself that'll make me sound datable. You know I'm terrible with this kind of thing." She shook her head at the screen.

I jumped down from the counter and took a look at the picture she'd added to her profile. It was a shot of her on a speedboat on Lake Michigan, taken when all of us—Mom, Dad, and me—had vacationed there years ago. "That's one of my favorite pictures of you." In the photo, she was squinting from the sunshine. Dad had called her name, and she'd turned with this natural, happy smile on her face.

It wasn't right that I was going to the beach today with Dad and the step-disappointments he'd forced into my life—Dad's new wife Barb and her son Craig. Being at the lake was supposed to be *our* family thing. It always used to be—and because of Mom. She'd get up early to organize bags of games and fill coolers with enough snacks to get us through a whole day.

"Is it too dated? You were, what, ten then?" Mom asked.

I nodded. That had been one of our best family trips ever. Instead of staying at a cheap motel, we'd camped, which meant I'd gotten to stay up late every night, roasting marshmallows and listening to their stories. I'd taken turns tubing with both Mom and Dad, scream-laughing our heads off. "You still look the same, except maybe your hair."

"I've really let it go, huh?" Mom pulled her fingers through the roots of her hair.

"Maybe it's time to fully accept your hair and go all silver."

Mom narrowed her eyes and pursed her lips for a second, deciding if I was kidding or not. "Hmm, I like it. Silver cougar."

"Ew, gross, Mom. Unless…you're into younger guys?"

Mom shrugged, giving me a mischievous look. "I hadn't considered it. But, thank you. Now I will."

"Again…ew. But for real, I'll help with this thing. Lemme see." I took her laptop and clicked to edit her bio.

"Is it weird having my daughter write my dating profile?"

"Yes. Yes, it is. But you are beautiful and kind and you deserve love." I kissed her cheek. "Mom, is that a tear in your eye?"

"Maybe. It's nice to hear. Thank you, sweetie."

"Well, it's not totally selfless. This service comes with the condition that I get a vote before any dates are made. You know, to weed out potential super-creepers."

She laughed. "Deal." A shy look crossed her face. "I actually have a date tonight. Heather set me up."

"For real? Whoa. That's exciting."

She shrugged again.

"Just let yourself have fun. No pressure."

I worked on her profile until a car horn honked. *Craig.* "Sorry, Mom. I'll finish this up later. The evil stepbrother is here." I kissed her good-bye, grabbed my bag, and hurried to the sliding-glass door.

"Be nice," she called after me. "Craig's a good boy."

A good boy? I resisted groaning out loud. Mom was bizarrely fond of Craig and invited him over to ruin our dinners several nights a week because she deemed it an injustice that my dad and his mom had moved to Wisconsin and abandoned him for more space and fresh cheese. His mom had gotten a dream job there, but this was Craig's senior year and he refused to leave. He argued that he was already eighteen and going to be on his own next year anyway, and somehow Barb let that fly.

As I fussed with the sticky sliding-glass door, Craig honked again. What the hell? Didn't he see me? I finally got the slider closed and headed for his car. In my rush, I stumbled over the edge of our "patio" (more accurately: "personal outdoor cement slab") and felt a sharp twitch above my knee. Jogging toward the passenger door I saw that, no, he couldn't have seen me standing there because he was looking down, elbow jammed into the steering wheel, scrolling through something on his phone.

I opened the door and got in.

"Nice Barbie Doll look," he said, pointing to my

straightened hair.

I pointed back at his thick, longish, wavy hair. "Nice Disney Princess look."

"Eat a bag." That was about the only comeback in his repertoire.

Craig Kowalski wasn't your average Northglenn senior. At six-foot-five he was the tallest guy in school who didn't play sports. He always wore a black leather jacket—and not in that bringing-back-the-eighties way. For real. He had dark hair, dark eyes, and an even darker soul.

Well, maybe he didn't have a dark soul, but he was a reminder of my parents' divorce and all that had gone wrong this summer with my dad getting remarried and moving out of state. Of course, Craig probably had it worse. At least I had my mom to depend on.

"Dude, you're sitting on my magic." He reached under my butt and started pulling out sheets of music I must have sat on.

I rolled my eyes. "Uh, your *magic*?"

Once his sheet music was in order, he said, "You wouldn't believe the tunes we laid down last night. Luke and I are gonna shake things up in the industry." And then he did his air guitar act. It really blew my mind that half the female population of our school swooned over him when he did that and said things like "tunes we laid down" in earnest.

"Good for you." I punched him on the shoulder. "Is this heart-to-heart over now?"

He clicked play on his phone, and out pumped music heavily laden with electronic synthesizer sounds. It started with a steady drumbeat, and then a kind of screechy-slidey violin was layered on top of that, followed by someone panting in short staccato breaths.

"What do you think?" He actually looked eager for my answer.

"It's really…different," I said, hoping a lukewarm response would end this conversation. No luck. He waited for more. "Honestly, those sounds made me uncomfortable."

"Exactly." He slammed his hand on the wheel, his face wild with enthusiasm. "That's what we're about, aggressively experimenting with how music can make you feel."

"You want people to feel an aversion to your music?"

"Well, not only that, but, yeah, we want people to be woken up by what we're creating."

"Won't it be hard to create a fan base like that?"

"It's *inspired*. I mean, the lame-ass music execs probably won't get into it, but Luke's got a buddy in the city who is friends with a guy at an independent label, so we're gonna bring this to him and try to get the underground appeal. Or, we'll stream it for free and create our own buzz. It'll connect people who are looking for an experience deeper than the pop crap designed to lull the masses."

I stared at him. "It's a million degrees out. I'm sweating. Can we just get to the beach?"

He clicked to the next track and finally drove out of the parking lot.

Each time a new track started he'd fill me in on the inner genius at play. I hoped for something that would make me feel *good*. But after five or six tracks, I gave up.

Craig's Barbie Doll remark grated on me. I had, quite recently, become one of *those* girls. One who spent an inordinate amount of time on her hair. And while it was hard for me to believe it had happened, I also couldn't get over how much better I looked. I'd regrettably received the skin-and-hair genes from the wrong side of the family. Instead of my mom's dewy skin and gleaming hair, I'd gotten my dad's blond, curly, dry DNA. Though my dad's genes were the recessive ones, they were infused with the cruel determination of our Viking heritage. Other than allowing me the one gift of slightly olive skin tone that kept me from burning every summer, the Scandinavian genes had viciously overpowered Mom's Italian perfection, leaving me with a frizzy, pale 'fro.

A few weeks ago, Mom somehow scraped together enough money to get me a top-of-the-line straightening iron as a gift for starting senior year. I tried the iron and fell in love with the transformation as my curls surrendered one by one. Thus, I became completely addicted to hair vanity. I started getting up thirty minutes early to blow out my curls and suppress them into a luminescent mane that, sadly, brought me more pride than my 4.0 GPA.

"Hey, nerdling, did you get totally tranced out from our sounds? That's kick-ass." Craig finally turned down the "music," and I snapped out of my reverie.

"No, I was in a deep meditative state, training my mind to be like a supple reed in the tortuous winds of your madness." I scrolled through his music, until I found a band called Lords of Misrule under his most-played list and risked it by pressing play.

"Good choice," he said. "I love this singer and her loop pedal wizardry."

I didn't know what a loop pedal was, but I was already smitten with the music. Not that I would share that fact. "Let's just get to the lake."

We pulled into the parking lot of Tower Beach, barely able to find a spot in the farthest corner. It was chaos. Our school had unjustly started two weeks ago in mid-August, but now it was Labor Day weekend, when everyone swarmed to the beach before it closed for the season. I prayed we wouldn't run into anyone from school while I was stuck with my pseudo-family.

On the plus side, Lake Michigan was looking particularly majestic with the sun sparkling against the soft waves. I couldn't wait to jump in and get a break from Craig, my family, and my undefined future.

On our way to the concession stand I waved at two sophomore girls who had done props for the *Music Man* last year when I played Marian the Librarian. We walked past members of Northglenn's swim team. And then, further down the beach, I recognized a few of the Porter improvisers we'd seen in Scared Scriptless last night. *What if Jason is here, too?* The possibility made me squirmy. I had to get him out of my head. It was one stupid improv scene. I couldn't let myself get all agitated over a guy I barely knew.

When we were almost at the snack stand, I stopped in my tracks. At the end of the line, pointing at the large menu above the counter, was Jason. He was with some beautiful girl with long silky hair who was wearing a tiny white bikini. White. Her hand was on Jason's shoulder, and she was leaning into him. My eyes froze open and a short grumble-moan escaped from my throat.

At least I was wearing the blue bikini Quinn brought back for me from her vacation in Greece this summer. She'd handed it to me then marched over to my dresser and stole all my full-piece swimsuits and said, "No more grandma suits for you," making it my only option for the family hangout today. Over the suit, I wore jean shorts and a thin white tank top so the plunging bikini top was still visible. It was no teeny white bikini, but better than my usual.

I grabbed Craig's arm to hold him back. "Hey, let's, um, go meet our parents first, then get snacks. See if they want any."

He looked to where my gaze had been. Crap. I was caught.

"What, you know them?" He looked back and forth between us. "Bet you have a thing for that guy, huh?" I rolled my eyes. He raised his eyebrows. They begged to be pulled out, hair by hair. "Now, Ellie, it'd be rude to ignore a friend."

"He's not a friend."

"A crush."

"No, I just…we…"

"Acquaintance? It's cool. I'll pretend for your sake that one of them is nothing more than an acquaintance. It's the girl you're into, then, isn't it?"

"You're impossible. I met that guy for a second at the show last night. Can we go now?"

"Of course not. It'd also be rude to ignore an acquaintance."

My Ice Princess glare did nothing because he pulled me into line, too close to Jason and his most-surely-a-model girlfriend.

They turned around at the same time. I can hardly explain the double take Jason gave me. It was like an emotional sundae—two scoops of fear with a sprinkle of *huh?* and a dollop of awkward with excitement on top.

"Wow, Ellie, hi. Crazy running into you. You guys took off so quickly last night I didn't get a chance to thank you for doing the show."

"Yeah, well, you know freshmen and their pesky curfews."

He nodded. I nodded back. *That torso.* Smooth and tan and apparently filled with a billion bio-magnets, because the entire organ that was my skin gravitated toward it.

Craig piped up, overenthusiastically, "Hey. I'm Craig, and you two are?"

"Sorry, sorry, hey, I'm Jason and this is Marissa."

"I heard you guys had some fun skits last night. That's so great," Marissa said. I winced at our improv set being called skits.

"Thanks, yeah, Scared Scriptless is a talented team. Very meshy and swirly," I said. Realizing how weird that must have sounded, I quickly added, "And funny."

Jason wore only his board shorts and flip-flops. I'd hoped my feelings last night were a result of the high from the show making everything shinier. But now, in the light of day, he looked even more irresistible than I remembered. Cheers and curses to the world of fashion for making low-riding board shorts a staple in guy's swimwear.

I wondered if Craig was having a similar fight to not look at Marissa's bikini-clad chest.

But he simply stared despondently at the menu choices.

I looked back at Jason. At the particular darkness of his choppy-but-not-shaggy brown hair, the way he rocked back and forth on his heels, and again at his shirtlessness. *Stop it. It's just a comedy crush. It'll pass.*

"So, did you see their show last night?" Marissa asked Craig.

He brought his eyes back from the menu and shook his head no.

"Yeah, me either. I mean, I think it's so great Jason and Mark and those guys can use their natural sense of humor, but I'm not a big fan of comedy. I'm more into the dramatic arts. Like Shakespeare and Brecht. That's what I do." She was trying to be nice, but made it sound like we were clowns with no actual skill involved in what we do. We just run around stage being our naturally wacky selves.

Craig nodded at her once and looked back up at the menu. For the first time, I wanted to hug him. You could tell Marissa was not used to this response from guys.

"We do an improv scene called Shakespeare," I said. "Where we make up a scene but speak as if we're in a Shakespearian play. Like..." Looking for inspiration, I pointed to the frozen yogurt machine and, affecting a dramatic British accent, said, "So soft, what delight through yonder fro-yo snakes?"

Marissa wrinkled her button nose, but Jason and Craig smiled, and I took it as a victory. Shifting her focus to Craig, Marissa said, "The guys are having a party at Jason's tonight. You two should come, right, Jason?"

"Definitely, of course, both of you should come." Jason

gestured to include Craig.

"Thanks, yeah. They mentioned that last night." I nodded, noncommittally. If that party was going to be a Marissa-Jason love fest, no thanks.

"The guys and I have a great spot on the beach. We could all…" Marissa pointed to the spot where they'd set up camp.

My eyes widened in horror. I tried to recover by matching her enthusiasm. "Oh that'd be great. But we're meeting our parents, so, we can't."

"Craig's your…brother?" Jason asked, looking back and forth between us.

Craig chuckled. "What, did you think me and Ellie were a thing? I could see how she might give off the vibe that she's totally hot for me, but of course, I wouldn't allow it. That would be so *wrong*, wouldn't it, *sis*?" He side-hugged me into him hard, squishing my cheek into his already-sweaty bare chest. *When did he take off his T-shirt?*

"It wouldn't be wrong. He's not my brother. I mean, it *would* be wrong, but not because of bloodlines. What I mean is, it would be spiritually, chemically, emotionally, physically wrong. Anyway. We better find our parents—one of his and one of mine. He's my stepbrother." With that Toast-Masters-worthy speech I wriggled out of his bear clasp and turned around. Then I turned back, remembering to be polite, gave a wave and added, "Bye."

Marissa gave me a confused, smiley look. Jason started to raise his hand like he was going to wave good-bye as I marched out of the snack stand. Craig followed.

"You say you perform? Maybe I should come see a show. Because if you're typically as eloquent as you were just now, I bet I would laugh a lot."

"Eat a bag, Craig."

"She's finally taking after her big brother."

I didn't even bother with my usual response to that

brother word. We trudged along looking for the purple plaid umbrella Barb had texted about.

After a few yards, Craig nodded back toward the snack stand. "What's with the meltdown over seeing those two?"

"Nothing." My flip-flops sank into the hot sand over and over again in rhythm—*trudge, lift, stomp, crush.* "They're just so beautiful and shiny and rich and sunny and full of perfectly perfect perfectness…and Jason and I had maybe the most mind-altering scene together I've ever had in improv—even though it was also incredibly embarrassing—but, of course, he has a kind and lovely girlfriend. It's nothing."

"Easy there, tiger. Those two are dating? You sure?" Craig walked leisurely, his long legs easily keeping pace with me.

"Yeah, I mean look at them." I flung my hand back, pointlessly gesturing at the snack stand.

"Yeah," he said, mimicking my tone. "I did. Hence, the question. They don't look like they're dating. And that Melissa girl was checking me out."

"Marissa," I corrected, not sure if she actually had checked him out and I should feel hopeful, or if that was just Craig speaking through his Craig-centric lens of life, where he assumed all girls were in love with him.

"I really did want a slushy," Craig grumbled.

Finally, the purple-and-green plaid umbrella stood before us. It was the worst umbrella ever, and I resisted a deep and desperate need to hurl it into the lake.

Further down the beach, my dad was kneeling in the sand close to the water building an elaborate wet-drip sandcastle complete with arches, turrets and bridges. I vowed to be nice to Barb. Maybe even Craig since he hadn't lost his brain around Marissa.

"Hey, you guys." Barb sprang from her lounge chair and scampered to us, which—due to the sand tripping her up— was hilarious. She was wearing a bright-purple, skirt-attached swimsuit with a visor that matched the umbrella. What kind of person matches her swimwear to her beach umbrella? Her curled, orangeish-brown-dyed hair puffed from the top of her visor like a crispy tumbleweed. Her cheeks were red from the heat. This was the woman who replaced my mother? *Don't glare, don't roll your eyes, don't tell her she deserves to be hurled into the lake with her aggressively obnoxious umbrella.*

"I'm so happy to see you two. Come here, big guy." She got on her tiptoes and planted several kisses on Craig's cheek. "I missed you."

He gave me a putout look, but you could tell by the way he hugged his mom back that he was happy to see her, too — just seriously more contained.

I was next. Barb hugged me so hard her floral perfume particles were already leaping onto my hair and clothes with a sticky vengeance. I would have to jump in the lake to get rid of the odor. How could my dad stand it?

"Ellie, you get more beautiful all the time. Isn't she just a stunner?"

This was exactly what annoyed me about Barb. She was the aspartame kind of sweet: promises of sweetness, but ultimately leaving you empty inside with a bad taste in your mouth. Look at her decision to abandon her son in his senior year. How many parents did Craig need to be abandoned by in one lifetime? And she'd revealed her true inner monster at the wedding when Dad wasn't looking — hollering at me because I'd spilled the stupid sparkling apple juice on my dress seconds before the ceremony.

I set my stuff down, kicked off my sandals, and joined Dad at his castle. He smiled, not taking his eyes off the tower-dripping procedure.

"Hey, Dad."

"Why, hello there, you."

More silence and wet-sand-dripping. I started making a

carriage house next to his castle. Okay, I guess I could have gone for *some* artificial sweetness. A pat on the upper arm maybe?

"Barb says you had a performance last night."

A. Why did she know and not him? B. Why didn't they drive down a day early to see it? C. Was this his way of asking how it went?

"I did." I waited for the appropriate follow-up question, but it didn't come. "It went really well, thanks for asking." He either didn't get the sarcasm, or he wasn't listening.

Drip. Drip. Drip.

The sunshine highlighted Dad's white hair. No traces of blond left. At least he still had a full, thick head of it.

"How are your new students?" I asked.

He looked at me for the first time since I got there. He seemed to have a whole new landscape of wrinkles. A grumbling noise came from the back of his throat. "Eh, there are fewer attitudes, and the maturity level is a welcome change."

He'd loved teaching at the prestigious private high school in Chicago, and it still baffled me that Barb had convinced him to move to Wisconsin, away from me and the job he loved.

My sand carriage house was looking more like a melted tomb. "Do you want to go for a walk along the beach?"

He clapped the sand from his hands. "Sure do."

We stood up, and he put his arm around me as we walked along the shore. This was more like it.

"How are the college applications coming along? Any chance we can get you at Madison? In-state potential there." University of Wisconsin did have a great biology program. But who knew if I really was going to major in that?

I wasn't about to tell him it wasn't even in the college pros-and-cons spreadsheet I was making. Taking in a deep breath of the warm Lake Michigan air, I gathered courage to tell him about my first choice. "I want to go to the University of Colorado at Boulder." I quickly added, "They have a highly-rated biology program. Plus, they have an improv group already established on campus."

"Ellie, you are not going to college for an extracurricular activity. It is time to focus."

I stuffed down the screams, moved out from under his arm, and went to skip a stone. I chucked it into the lake and it skipped along almost to where Marissa, Jason, Mark and some others from Porter were playing in the water—dunking, splashing, laughing—like a freaking sunscreen commercial.

"Dad, I forgot to put on sunscreen, let's head back."

We walked back in silence. I grunted at Barb and Craig, flopped down on the blanket, and put my shirt over my face. The Freeze scene with Jason replayed in my mind, but this time there wasn't an audience, and in the final moment when I was hovering over him onstage, instead of laughing—

"Ellie? Are you under there?"

Holy crap. I bolted upright, throwing the shirt off my face, trying to smooth my hair in a casual way.

"Jason? Hi," I said, overanimated, feeling like he must be able to guess my reverie about him.

"Hey. I figured as long as we were a few hundred yards from each other on the same beach, I could give you the info for my party tonight now?" He said this as a question, his face crinkling up in the most adorable way. The sun was at his back so he looked like he was glowing—his hair shimmering, droplets of water running down his face. *No fair providing special effects, Nature.*

"Yeah, that'd be great, thanks." I reached for my phone. He kneeled down next to me, his thigh brushing against mine. It took all my focus to enter in his address, my thumbs forgetting how to type.

He smiled, his dimple a talented wingman. "I really

hope you can make it," he said as he stood back up, leaving a noticeable absence on the spot where his leg had pressed into mine.

My words left along with his touch. I nodded instead, realizing there had been a lightning-quick debate between my body and my brain, and my body had won. *There's no way I'm missing this party.*

Chapter Three

When we arrived at Jason's palatial home, cars lined the street and driveway, including Craig's. He'd driven separately so he could escape early in case it turned out to be an "actor freakfest of sucky proportions." We found a spot to park, got out and gave each other one final glance over. Quinn wore a black tutu-like skirt and nude high heels, a combo that made her long, athletic legs look endless. Hana had tried to wear one of her adorable-things-in-nature T-shirts but Quinn wouldn't stand for it. Instead of the river-with-cute-jumping-fish shirt, she now wore a royal-blue short-sleeved sweater that for once showed off her ample boobs instead of hiding them under layers of cotton.

My original outfit had also been rejected, Quinn saying, "You need to show off that new yoga body."

"Uh, I've only been doing yoga for the two weeks since school started," I'd said.

"Well, you look stronger and glowier already. Own it." She forced me to trade out my usual gray canvas shoes for shiny gold flats and had me put on her silky, cream-colored top that danced around my skin.

While Quinn tousled my hair and applied my makeup with her expert skills, Hana decided it would help if she assigned me a character for the night. "Tonight, you're playing the part of Girl Who's Got It All. I mean, be yourself, but only that witty, confident part of you who can actually talk to the cute boy, and not that weirdo part of you who sees a cute boy, mumbles something unintelligible and runs to her friends at her first chance. Got it?" Since I'd had a stick of eyeliner pointed at my eyeball, I couldn't glare at her, but I liked my assignment. *Tonight's performance of Confident Girl will be played by Ellie Hartwood.*

After checking that my blouse was hanging just so over my jeans, we headed up the driveway to Jason's ginormous house.

Hana nudged Quinn and said, "So, which guy is on your hump-worthy list tonight?"

"Well, I certainly don't like considering it that way," Quinn said, trying to get away with not answering. She enjoyed flirting but never really stuck with a crush for very long. We remained silent, expectant. "*C'est un mystère.*" She punctuated the statement with a quick nod of her head.

We stopped and blocked her path, staring at her for an answer.

Finally, she broke. "Okay, I kind of think that Mark Weiss guy is cute. And he was so funny last night."

"Yuck. Seriously?" Hana was never good at hiding her opinions, even when hiding them was the right thing to do.

"What? *Mean.*" She turned to me. "Is that what you think, too?"

Liberated by Hana's response I tried to be honest. "You're right, he is funny, and his smile could land him some toothpaste commercials, no doubt, but…he's so bizarrely tan."

"Yeah, he's kinda the color of Cheetos."

"You guys. He is *not* orange." Quinn flung her hands up in the air.

Hana and I exchanged sidelong glances.

For a moment, Quinn was all the image of innocence and hurt, but she soon gave in. "Well, he is slightly…marigold-colored, but—"

All three of us burst out laughing.

"I still call dibs. If the Weisses don't vacation in Florida anytime soon or have a tanning booth in their basement, I'm sure the color will wear off by Homecoming."

"Ooh, she's got *plans,*" Hana teased.

I elbowed Hana in the side. "So, how about you, Hana? Got your eye on anyone?"

She made an odd, quiet grunt.

"Is there someone?" Quinn asked.

Hana shook her head and frowned, avoiding eye contact. "Nah, these Porter guys aren't for me."

Something in the way she emphasized *Porter* guys made me wonder. "Okay, so no Porter guys for you. But *is* there someone you like?" I did a skip-jump to get in front of her and read her face. *Oof.* My knee twinged in the spot I'd tweaked this morning.

She shrugged, her head kind of bobbling between yes and no.

"You're never rendered speechless. Who?"

"Yes, who? Do tell," Quinn said as she took Hana by the shoulders and looked real close at her face, as if the boy's name might be written there.

"Okay, okay. There is a guy—"

Quinn and I squealed in unison, our mouths opening like baby birds about to demand more.

"But." Hana stomped her foot, her heel making a loud click against the brick. "And I'm serious here. For reasons I don't want to go into, I'm asking, as your best friend, please do not press me on this. I'm hoping this uncomfortable emotion will just go away, but if it doesn't I promise I will tell you soon. Okay?"

I put my hand over my mouth, trying to squelch my desire to ask a hundred more questions. This was so unlike her I was almost in shock. Quinn squirmed next to me. We were all silent for a long beat until I sighed and said, "Well, I've never been more curious in all my life. It's pretty much all I'm going to think about for forever until you tell us."

"A week," Quinn said.

"What?" Hana asked.

"You have to tell us in at least a week, or our brains will explode. You understand."

Hana nodded, and we continued up the long driveway bordered with inlaid bricks and motion-sensor lights. My belly did a flip thinking about my own crush, whom I was about to see in two seconds. *Are he and Marissa together? Or is Craig right, and there isn't anything between them?*

As Quinn opened the front door, I gaped at the stained-glass panels refracting shimmers of colorful light. This house was a gazillion times different then our apartment, where the only thing shiny was the glitter stucco ceiling leftover from a tragic eighties remodel. I was luckier than 95 percent of the world's population, but except for a handful of apartment-living kids in unincorporated Northglenn like Hana and me, everyone else in our school had huge houses. They were fancy-summer-camps and vacation-homes rich. And then there were neighborhoods like this one, with inconceivable amounts of money. I tried to shake it off—comparing up sucked.

This place was something else entirely. As if reading my mind, Hana said, "Yeah, I think the word for this is *estate.*"

From down the marble-floored hall a voice shouted, "The party's out back!" We walked down the hall toward this mysterious "back." Hana muttered, "They should offer a shuttle service. I'm getting shin splints."

We stopped at a room filled with boys yelling at a video game on a TV so big it rivaled a movie theater. Some of them were wearing headsets that looked like half-helmets. Quinn, Hana, and I just stared at them and the screen where soldier types were killing monster types.

"We've made a huge mistake," I whispered.

In another corner of the room, Craig was holding a guitar and Jason was talking and pointing to some other music equipment. I didn't know what I thought about them being chummy. Oh, wait, yes, I did—I didn't like it.

Jason looked up and walked over. "You made it. Hi." He said this to all three of us, but his focus was on me, his eyes causing all sorts of spasms and palpitations in my organs.

"Hi." I could think of no other words. *Don't I do improv? Why does it refuse to be a useful skill in real life?*

"Took long enough," Craig said. He looked at me, Quinn then Hana, and waved his hand around at us as he said, "You three look…nice. *Effortful,* but nice." His eyes landed on Hana's cleavage for a millisecond, which surprised me since our beach run-in with Marissa had made me think his resistance was stronger than the normal teenage male in the boob-gawking department.

"Something to drink?" Jason asked. He waved for us to follow him as he listed drink options too quickly for me to catch.

"I was about to bring these out back." Jason started pulling large glass bottles of some fancy soda out of the fridge. Who knew pulling out bottles of soda could highlight a butt so nicely?

"Here," Quinn stepped into the kitchen and reached for the bottles. "Hana, Craig, and I can take these outside for you." She hoisted three of them into Craig's arms, took the other four for her and Hana, and backed out of the kitchen.

"We'll see you outside."

Jason pointed in the opposite direction from where we'd entered. "Just go down the hall then take a left through the library to the backyard."

Hana mouthed to Quinn, "the *library*?" as they skittered away without me. Clearly, my friends had purposely abandoned me.

I smiled awkwardly at Jason.

He smiled handsomely back at me.

Think, Ellie, think. "Your line last night, 'It smells like Fig Newtons and desperation,' was brilliant, by the way."

"Ha. Thanks, I don't know where that came from." He shifted his weight and crossed his arms over his chest. "I couldn't stop laughing at your Little Miss Princess scene with Quinn."

He remembers my character.

He thinks I'm funny.

"I have to ask. *How* did you keep your upper lip folded against your teeth the whole time?" He tried to mimic what I had done and looked so silly—flaring his nostrils trying to get his upper lip to stay folded under—that I laughed.

"The key is to get your teeth dry first. It works best when you're severely dehydrated." I tucked my upper lip under to show him.

He laughed. "That talent is going to get you far. Though, I hope you're not severely dehydrated now. Do you want any of that sparkling stuff?"

I unfolded my lip. "Plain ol' water would be great, thanks."

He got a glass and turned to fill it in the refrigerator door. "Your brother is a talented guitar player."

Stepbrother, I managed to not correct aloud. "So he tells me." *Not much better.* "Do you play?"

"He used to," a voice said from behind me.

"Ellie, this is my sister Olivia. She goes to Northwestern so she could stay at home," Jason said with a warmth I wouldn't have suspected from a younger brother. "Olivia, this is Ellie. She's from Northglenn's improv group."

"Hello, Ellie. You must be good. Jason never invites the other improv groups over." Olivia was rocking the sexy librarian look—black glasses, crisp clothes, tight bun and all. She shook my hand, hers petite and bony in mine. "Jason's guitar playing was decent, but his singing, wow. 'The voice of an angel,' Mom would say. But he hasn't done any of that in forever." She gave him a faraway look.

Jason winced. "I wasn't that good."

"He was." Olivia smiled, which made her eyes look just like Jason's. She gave him a kiss on the cheek. "I'm off. Dad is in his office. I told him not to leave it until everyone is gone, so be good and don't destroy the house, m'kay? Nice to meet you, Ellie."

She clicked away in her shiny shoes. *I hope there is some magical thing that happens automatically between high school and college that will make me look that confident and together by next year.*

Jason led the way outside, and as we stepped out onto the brick patio, I let out a little gasp at the gorgeous gardens over the expanse of their yard.

"Did I mention Olivia is studying botany? She wants to eventually get a doctorate in pharmacognosy."

"What's that?"

"Basically, how plants can be turned into medicine. She's obsessed with the idea of curing a rare disease, but I think she's an artist at heart." Jason gestured out to the gardens.

"She's definitely that." The yard was filled with winding stone paths, bonsai trees, intricate bushes, and flowers everywhere. "It's amazing. Looks straight out of the Japanese gardens at the Chicago Botanic Garden."

There were shrieks of laughter. Quinn, Hana, Craig, and

the curly-haired guy from the Porter team, Owen, who had hosted the show, hovered over Quinn's phone with bewildered looks on their faces.

"This is the best thing I've ever seen," Hana said.

Jason and I squeezed into the group and Quinn raised her phone up so we could see what they were watching. It was a Spanish music video that looked to be from the seventies, with upbeat music and trilling flutes. The lead singer sported a sparkly bellbottomed jumpsuit, and the chorus of singers and dancers behind him wore their own shiny jumpsuits with glittery stars stuck on their clothes and in their hair.

"Is that floating guy trying to dance like a bird? What's with the star-spangled bikini lady?" Owen doubled over with laughter.

Jason and I started laughing, too.

"That is a mind-blowing fusion of Spanish music and Dutch fashion," Jason said.

I pointed at the front man with the dark, feathery bouffant. "Craig, you look like the lead singer."

"Eat a bag."

"Omigosh, if we just feathered your hair and got you a gold jumpsuit, I could totally see it, Craig," Quinn added.

"Does anyone know what they're singing about?" I asked.

"*Una paloma blanca*," Hana said. "A white dove."

"Yeah," Jason said, "he's singing, 'No one can take my freedom, I fly free over the mountain top. No one can take my power, I'm just a bird in the sky.'" He translated as the group of dancers, after several attempts, lifted one guy over their heads and flew him around as he flapped his arms like wings.

Owen was crying he was laughing so hard now. "We should…" He took his glasses off and wiped his eyes. "We should parody this as a sketch for the Comedy Hub contest."

"My family could totally help make the costumes," Quinn said.

"And Craig can be our lead Spaniard." Hana elbowed Craig in the side.

"Aw, hell no," Craig said.

Owen and Jason pointed to each other. Owen said, "You speak Spanish," at the same time Jason said, "You're taller."

"Anyway, I don't think this can be parodied, it's already too ridiculous as is," Jason said.

"This has to be done. Even if we just straight up recreate it. The modern world needs to see this," Owen said as the whole chorus of singers and dancers flocked around bending their knees and flapping their arms. "Would you all really be up for doing this with us?" He looked directly at Quinn as he asked this, like she was a real-life goddess. I wondered if he stood a chance with her against Marigold-Mark.

Hana, Quinn, and I looked at each other and were in instant agreement. "Definitely," Quinn answered for all of us, as I got giddy imagining the weeks ahead hanging out with Jason to rehearse this spectacle.

"Okay, let's do it then," Jason said. "Craig, do you think you'd be able to recreate this music track with your equipment?"

Craig gave a solid nod, which in his native Neanderthal translated to, "Yeah, sure."

My giddy feeling diminished as the vision of the weeks ahead changed into hanging out with Jason...and my annoying stepbrother.

The other members of Spontaneous Combustion were by a patio table with snacks. Quinn, Hana, Owen, and Craig headed over to join them, which meant Jason and I were left alone again.

Music started playing over the outdoor speakers, and I jumped at the noise.

Jason yelled over the music. "You okay?"

"Yeah, I'm fine, that just surprised me. I'm intrigued to

see if we can pull off this Spanish seventies dove number."

"I know. Any chance you play the flute?"

The music got even louder.

"No, but I'm told I'm *quite talented* at pretend-playing the flute," I said with mock pride.

"Excellent." He smiled. "Hey, you guys should do another Mash-Up, too. We just had a group cancel on us for the next one, if you're free."

"I'll check, but I'm sure they're up for it. It was great to play for so many people—we never get crowds like that at Northglenn."

We listened to the loud thumping music.

I took a sip of water.

"Not to sound—" The bass beat garbled up Jason's words.

"What? Sorry, I missed that."

"Do you want to walk over there where it's quieter?" Jason lightly grabbed my elbow to lead me to the other end of the house where we walked up a few stairs to the deck. All the parts of my body that weren't my elbow were jealous.

"What were you saying?" I asked when we stopped. I set my water glass on one of the flat wooden rails.

"I was just saying, not to sound cheesy, but that scene we had together last night was…I don't know…that level of being in sync, it was cool. I've never done something like that before."

I decided to be honest, since he was. "Same. It was practically an out-of-body experience, but not, because I was completely in it, you know?" I turned to him. Dangerous move, considering those eyes of his.

"Exactly," he said in a way that sent sparks dominoing along my limbs.

We looked around the yard as if there were something important we had to find out there.

"So, is Marissa here?" *Subtle.*

He looked confused. "Marissa?"

"Yeah, the girl you were with at the beach?"

"Ah right, Mark's girlfriend."

"Mark's girlfriend? I thought you two were together."

He laughed. "No girlfriends for me. Those two have been together forever. There she is, with Mark." He pointed across the yard to an area of patio couches that surrounded a fire pit.

Marissa and Mark were on the couches wrapped in each other's arms, and Quinn was there, too, looking mighty cozy with Owen. What a difference two minutes could make.

Waiting to get control over my giant smile, I absently ran my finger along an engraved pattern in the deck rail.

"I love this detail on the rail," I said, tracing the smooth loops in the wood.

His voice got quiet. "My dad loves it, too. It means a lot to him."

"The railing? Why?"

Jason looked out at the darkness of the yard. He glided his finger along the pattern in the rail like I had.

"My mom commissioned the project after she got really sick."

My stomach sank. "I'm so sorry. Is she okay?"

"She wanted a nice place to sit outside that was higher up so she could see all of her and Olivia's gardens while she recovered. But she didn't get to enjoy it for very long. She passed away last year."

I didn't know why I got so emotional about a person I'd never met, but tears welled in my eyes.

What do you say? What are you supposed to say?

"My dad had this detail added to the railing after she was gone, as kind of a memorial to my mom. The engraving looks like a flower pattern, but if you look closely, it's her name — Linda May — written over and over again along the entire rail. After it was finished, I found my dad holding on to the railing later that night, crying. I hadn't seen him like that since she died."

We both stared silently at the carving. Hugging my arms across my body, I tried to speak, but Jason started first.

"Sorry, that was probably way too much. I don't usually talk about my mom with people." He laughed uneasily. "When you mentioned the engraving, it just came out."

"No, no. I'm so sorry, Jason," I said, looking up, finally finding my words. "You seem to be doing... I don't know. I guess people learn how to act strong, but—"

"It's been over a year now, and I'm doing better. Last year I was a total mess. Now I'm only an occasional mess."

I nodded. *C'mon words.* Here he was spilling his life to me, and all I could do was nod.

"Hey, that's a good reason for not wanting a girlfriend for the last year, right?" He lifted his hands to the side and let out another awkward laugh.

My stomach sank another inch. *When he said "no girlfriends for me," he didn't mean "at the moment," he meant it as a policy. Got it.* "It makes sense considering all you've been through."

"I didn't think I could do improv again, either, but it helps." Jason crossed his arms over his chest, mirroring me. "It's nice to escape and be someone else for a while."

"I get that escaping part. I love that about improv." I paused. "I don't know what to say, Jason, I'm so sorry."

"Thanks. Man, *I'm* sorry I went into all that."

"Don't be sorry. I just wish I could put all your heartache into a big bag and take it to the beach with me for a day so you could have a break from it."

"That's nice. I like that." The smile came back to his face. He looked at me for a while before continuing. "And the other good part of doing improv is I got to meet you, right?" His voice was soft as he reached out like he was about to touch my arm.

He doesn't want to have a girlfriend, but he's glad he got to meet me? What does that mean?

Jason's face changed, and he coughed a little, his arm continuing past mine and pointing behind me. "Well, it's not a beach, but there's a nice fire going out there. Sound good?"

I nodded and headed toward the others. Before stepping down off the deck, I remembered my drink on the rail. As I turned back to get it, I was stopped by the wall of Jason's torso, his chest rising and falling beneath my palms and his thin T-shirt. *Maybe he won't notice if I stay here forever.*

But as I stepped to steady myself, my left foot slipped from the deck to the step below, landing with a forceful jolt. There was a horrific *snap* as my leg crumpled beneath me. So much pain. A guttural cry pushed itself out of me as I tumbled down the stairs, my head smacking against something hard before my body landed with a thud on the earth.

Chapter Four

I was in a hospital room, aching from temples to eyeballs like there was a vise grip around my skull. A man in scrubs futzed with an IV next to me, and Quinn and Hana were on my other side, their faces stricken with fear. *Well, that's comforting.*

The nurse said, "Hi, Ellie, I'm your nurse, Jim." He had a drawl and the bushiest mustache I'd ever seen.

Aside from the pain, or maybe because of it, I felt drunk and loopy, even though I hadn't had a single drink. "Hi. Is my leg a broken disaster? It made a snapping sound."

Jim gave me a smile. "We took some X-rays, and the doctor will let us know soon." He gave me a reassuring pat.

I winced at Hana and Quinn. "You guys, never take me to a party again. That was the most embarrassing exit of anyone ever in the history of party exits."

Quinn squeezed my hand. "The whole thing was crazy. I'm so glad you're okay. Jason started yelling for someone to call 911, and we found you in a heap on the lawn. It was by far the most terrifying thing I've ever seen."

"That's because you don't keep up on the news." Through

narrow slits of my eyelids, I saw her frowning at me.

"If catapulting off a patio is your way of getting out of making out with a boy, for future reference, you don't have to be so dramatic," Hana said.

"I *did* want to make out with a boy. With Jason. And…"

"Jason," Quinn said, "was adorable."

"Adorable," Hana seconded.

Quinn went on. "You should have seen how he took charge. People went to try to move you, but he said to leave you in case there was any issue with your neck—you landed in a messed-up way. Marissa said he's a lifeguard so he knows this stuff. He had Owen get a blanket from the living room. 'Not the wool one, the soft one,' he ordered."

I vaguely remembered some of this, and especially remembered Jason saying it was all his fault as he wrapped me in the blanket and held my hand until the paramedics came.

"Serious Prince Charming crap he did with you," Hana said. "If I hadn't been so scared, I would have puked at the sweetness." She pretended to gag.

Quinn sighed. "After you left in the ambulance, he said he was going to come to the hospital as soon as he could get everyone out of the house."

"He's coming here? Where he'll see me like…" I gestured to the hospital bed and my aching head.

"You look fine, just a bit…mangled. Do you want me to call him and tell him not to come?" Quinn asked, her eyes alight with worry.

I was torn. *See Jason again? Yes, please. Here, like this? No, thank you.* "Make up something good?"

"I can do that," Quinn said.

"Thanks. Hey, did anyone call my mom?" I asked.

Quinn nodded. "Craig called her as they were getting you into the ambulance, but she was on a date in the city, so it's going to take her a little longer. She should be here any minute."

"Oh yeah, the guy Aunt Heather set her up with. Of course, the one night she goes on a date in decades, and I have a catastrophe." My head pounded.

"Craig's getting some snacks from the vending machine. He'll be back soon." Hana perked up a little. She said this as if he were the greatest hero in all Chicagoland.

Quinn and I glanced at each other with wide eyes, then to Hana, and said, "It's *Craig*."

I sat up, blood sloshing through my brain, and said, "Holy crap. You're in love with *my stepbrother*?"

Hana's entire face flushed pink, and she quickly covered it with both hands. "I'm not in *love*." She made that word sound like something disgusting. "He's just so...so...tall. And he plays the guitar like a god—"

Quinn doubled over laughing. As I laughed, I pounded my fist into the bed because it hurt my head to laugh so hard, but I couldn't help it.

Quinn recovered somewhat and pried Hana's hands apart so she could look at her directly. "Hana Yoon, did you just say he plays guitar *like a god*? Who *are* you?"

"Shut up, you guys." Hana clenched her fists by her sides, her face now more the color of a pomegranate. And that was the moment Craig chose to open the door and march in, looking more frazzled than I'd ever seen him, his arms spilling over with bags of chips and cookies. "Aaahh!" Hana screamed. She actually *screamed,* and then, mumbling, she ran past Craig out the door, the only intelligible word being "bathroom."

"Do you want a snack?" Craig called after her.

Hana's hand reached from behind the door, snatched a package of cookies, and slipped back out again.

Quinn grabbed a bag of pretzels from Craig and showed me the phone to confirm she'd complete her Jason-mission before she followed Hana out the door.

Craig surveyed the room like he wasn't sure what just happened. "You girls are the weirdest. What was up with Hana?"

It took all my strength as a friend to stifle my laughter and Hana's big secret. Thankfully, I was saved from having to answer his question because Mom arrived.

She rushed to the bed and kissed my forehead and cheeks repeatedly. "What happened, are you okay, sweet pea? I'm so sorry it took me so long to get here." To Craig she said, "Thanks for calling."

He nodded.

She bent down to give me a big hug and whispered softly in my ear, "My sweet baby, I love you so much."

This was what I needed—Mom hugs. If my leg wasn't broken, why was I still here? "Sorry I ruined your big date. How was it?"

She pulled back from the hug and waved away my concern. She'd dyed her hair—her usual brown—and she was wearing a soft, green sweater. "Actually, sweetie, you *saved* me. I just wish it wasn't because of this." She gestured the length of the hospital bed.

"Really? Why?"

"Stupid man couldn't stop talking about how much money he makes and how his ex is a B-I-T-C-H who was trying to steal it all from him. Real romantic. Won't be doing that again for a while."

On the other side of the room, measuring his height on the metal scale, Craig said, "C'mon, Sonia, you can't let one jerk keep ya down. I dare you to date three more giant douchebags so you can get them out of the way."

Mom laughed. "I don't know, we'll see. Anyway, who cares right now. I'm just glad you're safe."

There was one firm knock on the door, and then a doctor

burst into the room, his eyes darting between Mom and me like he wasn't sure who to talk to first. He had a whole mad-scientist look about him.

Hana and Quinn slipped back into the room.

The doctor strode over to my mom and me. "Hello, I'm Dr. Springfield. Are you the patient's mother?"

"I am. And her name is Ellie."

"Yes, of course. Hello, Ellie." He gestured at Craig, Quinn, and Hana all huddled in the corner. "This is a rather large group. Would you like me to wait for anyone who's not family to leave before presenting the news?"

Mom gave me a look that told me it was my choice.

"News? That's ominous." I laughed like this was a good joke. *Why so serious?* "No, I want my friends here. They can stay."

Dr. No-People-Skills disapproved. Or maybe his face always looked like that. "All right then." He threw the X-rays up onto a light box and flipped on the switch to illuminate them. "The good news is, you didn't break or even fracture the bone, which, considering how much the bone has weakened, and the nature of your fall, is surprising. However—"

"What do you mean the bone has weakened?" My mom gripped my hand tightly and stood up. "How? Why has it weakened?"

"Yes, I was getting to that." Dr. Assface pointed to a spot on the long thighbone on the scan, about two inches above my knee. "See, here on the femur. This area here appears to be a tumor."

"A tumor?" Mom asked, incredulous.

"Most likely an enchondroma. A benign bone tumor that originates from cartilage. It could even be a bone spur, but due to the apparent weakness in the bone, you will have to stay overnight so we can get a better look at it in the morning. We'll order scans for tomorrow."

My body froze, except for my heart, which was beating too fast.

"I'm sorry, I don't understand. How could I have a tumor, an enchon—whatever it is? I'm only seventeen." It was all I could think to say.

Dr. No-Bedside-Manners gave the air of zero-time-to-explain. "Yes, they're rare in someone your age, but that's why it's most likely benign."

"*Most likely* benign?" Mom asked as her eyebrows shot up her forehead.

Those words. *Tumor. Benign.* They blew through my center like a cartoon cannon ball, leaving a hole where my stomach used to be.

"Yes. We'll need a better look. An oncologist will meet you in the morning. They'll move you to an inpatient bed soon. Mrs. Hartwood, if you could fill this out?" He handed Mom a tablet.

She took it, looking at the doctor as if she might bludgeon him with it as he walked out the door. I wished she would. Mom examined the tablet like the writing was in a foreign language, practically tossed it down on the chair, and came to the side of my bed where Quinn and Hana had already flocked to me. Craig lurked behind them with his head down, hands in his leather jacket.

Quinn started, "Ellie, this is crazy." She squeezed my hand, and I didn't squeeze it back, on account of my center being blown through and making me immobile. Her eyes started to well up. "Whatever this is—"

"Dr. Assface is the worst. He doesn't know what he's talking about." Anger brought energy back to my limbs, and I took my hand back from Quinn, squashing the bed sheet between my fists. I needed everyone to leave. "Anyway, all he did know is that if it's anything, it's nothing. Benign. So, I'm fine. You don't have to worry about me, but thanks."

They stared at me like maybe I'd hit my head harder than they realized.

"Craig, girls," Mom said, putting a hand on my shoulder. "Ellie's already had a very long night. Clearly we're not going to get any answers out of…Dr. Assface. So, I think it would be best if you three head home, and we all get some sleep."

"Of course," Quinn said with a sincere smile. "You're right about that doctor. He's the worst."

"Capital D Douchebag," Craig added.

"My guess is he's on drugs," Hana said and leaned down to give me a hug. "Call us the second you hear anything tomorrow."

Quinn gave me a hug next. "Love you, Ellie."

Craig didn't fight his way around Quinn and Hana to give me a hug but just gave a small wave and said, "Night, sis," being the one person I could count on to not make a big deal out of this. Who knew Craig would ever come in handy?

They trudged out the door and Mom followed them, telling me she was going to see about the room transfer. The quiet of the room hit me, the outline of my legs under the thin sheet looming like a ghost. I shut my eyes and pressed my fists hard against my forehead, breathing deep through my nose, trying to keep the tears at bay.

Chapter Five

I woke up to loud knocks on the door and the overhead lights blaring cruelly bright. Disoriented, my eyes squinted open, blinking to adjust. *This is real. I'm really in the hospital.* Sheets twisted, skin clammy, head throbbing, I gasped for air and scrambled to sit up.

My phone slipped down the blanket. I'd fallen asleep with it clutched to my chest. When we'd settled into the new room the night before, I got a text from Jason.

> *Quinn told me no more visitors. :(I promise I didn't mean to scare you down the stairs. Can I see you tomorrow?*

I read it over and over before falling asleep with it in my hand. *Can I see you tomorrow?* It'd been the one glimmer of hope in my surreal night. I should be paralyzed with embarrassment from my tumble and tragic party departure, but here I was in a hospital bed, in ugly pink pajamas Mom had found at the gift shop, so my emotional capacity for embarrassment was lower than usual. *Hey, thanks, possible tumor, for giving me that.* Was he about to kiss me last night? He wouldn't have texted if he didn't care.

Mom stirred in the cot next to me as a doctor strode into the room and stood impatiently by my bedside. I glanced at the clock: 5:04 a.m. *So not nice.* Had this doctor missed the section in med school about the healing power of sleep? The poster on the wall behind the clock was of snow-capped mountains with the words *Indomitable Spirit* written on the bottom, like a threat.

"Good morning. I'm Dr. Nichols, your oncologist." She wore a white doctor's coat and her black hair pulled back into a bun. With a quick glance at her clipboard she said, "Nice to meet you, Ellie," and then shook my hand so firmly I wondered if I'd have to stay in this room another night for crushed finger bones. A plump older nurse trailed in behind her and introduced herself as Darlene.

"Mrs. Hartwood?" Dr. Nichols said.

"Please, call me Sonia." Mom rose awkwardly from her cot, still dressed in her clothes from the night before, and came to stand next to me at the head of my bed, rubbing her eyes.

"I examined the X-rays, and we definitely need to get a better look. Ellie, today you will get blood work done and a series of scans," Dr. Nichols said as the grandma nurse tapped away on her tablet. "MRI, bone scan, and CT scan with and without contrast. We'll also want to schedule a biopsy as soon as I have an opening."

"A biopsy? What do you think it is? Dr. Springfield told us it's probably benign, that it could just be a bone spur," Mom said.

Dr. Nichols shook her head. "It's not a bone spur. There is a chance the tumor is benign. The scans and biopsy will give us a more precise picture of its depth and location. Until we know more, Ellie, I don't want you running, jumping, or doing anything that could put too much force on your leg."

"What? I—I don't understand." Mom shook her head, eventually finding more words. "What do you think it is? Does it look malignant? What happens if she does accidentally put too much pressure on it?"

A hundred mini boa constrictors flooded my throat, tightening and squeezing, suffocating my voice and breath.

"I'm sorry. We can't answer most of those questions until we get a better look. The physical limitation is just a precaution. If the tumor is malignant and Ellie were to fracture or break the bone, it would make our treatment options more complicated. Don't think too much about it. It's a precaution." And with that, Dr. Nichols left.

That was it. No more reassuring words, just "don't think about it."

That seemed impossible. But she'd said there was a chance it was benign. *I have to hold on to that, to think only of that.*

The gripping coils in my nerves just rooted deeper. Relief would only come with an answer.

At least, I prayed it would be relief.

"We'll be doing the MRI after the blood work," said Nurse Darlene. She handed me a mint-green gown. "Please put this on with the opening in the back, dear, and make sure to take off your bra and any jewelry. We don't want any metal in the machine. I'll wait for you in the hall."

Mom's face matched the fear that was coursing through me. This was all happening too fast. No discussion, no satisfying explanations.

She gave me a kiss on the forehead. "I'm going to go talk to the nurse for a minute." She smoothed her bedhead down then held my chin and kissed my forehead again before leaving.

Once I had on the gown, I tried to wrap the flaps to cover my back and tuck them under me as I sat on the edge of the bed.

I should be at Quinn's—still asleep—making banana pancakes in a few hours. What is going on?

I glared at the mocking mountain picture and imagined my indomitable spirit ripping it off the wall and smashing it to the ground with my indomitable strength.

There was a tap at the door. Craig. He set down the bag of stuff that Mom had asked him to bring from our apartment and sat next to me on the bed. "So, a tumor, huh? That sucks."

A single "ha" slipped out of me. It wasn't what I was expecting him to say at all. "Yeah." I gave a sad smile.

He simply looked back at me. A choky feeling rose up in my throat. He surprised me by wrapping his arms fully around me and hugging me tight. I realized it was the first time we'd really hugged, and it went on and on.

What is he doing? But then, it was the nicest sort of hug. He held me so tight and so close, it was kind of comforting. Brotherly.

Tears streamed down my face, my body shaking against his. He was so big, and I felt so small. I had no idea how I'd get the tears and the shaking to stop now. Craig squeezed me tighter, and finally I put my arms around him and hugged him back.

"It's okay, little bird, it's okay," he whispered.

I was a little broken bird.

When Craig was gone Mom came back into the room shaking her head. "The nurse says your MRI will take an hour or so, and that I can't go with you." She scanned my eyes like they'd reveal if I'd be okay, and gave me a long, too-tight hug that told me she might not be.

Darlene pushed me in a wheelchair down the antiseptic-smelling hall. Would this be my future? A wheelchair forever? *Don't be ridiculous.*

I willed myself to go through the motions. *Needle prick, filling vials—one, two, three—dots of blood, press the gauze. You can do this. Get through today.*

The MRI room was cold, with a monolith of a machine in the middle of the room. It stood higher than I was tall and was more than twice as long, with a deep, cylindrical hole at its center. At the entrance, there was a bed-pod of sorts.

The technician, Troy, who seemed like he should be surfing on the California coast instead of working in this high-tech room of bad news, cinched straps around my ankles. Troy explained to me the importance of the straps. "Is this all right? Not pinching?"

"I know I'm in here because of a tumor and everything, but I have to ask, how do you get your curls to stay shiny and curly but not look scrunchy?"

His raised an eyebrow and smiled. "My secret is I don't wash with shampoo. Ever."

"For real?"

"For real. Only once in a while with baking soda and apple cider vinegar."

"Whoa, I love shampoo. I don't know if I could ever be that strong. Also, fair warning, you better pull those straps tighter or I'm gonna bolt."

He chuckled and gave a good show of pulling the straps imperceptibly tighter. "I'm going to go ahead and guess you are strong enough." He grinned, patted me on the shin and handed me some earplugs. "It's pretty noisy when the machine gets going. These will help. If you need anything over the next hour there's a microphone here so I'll be able to hear you. No need to be scared."

Yeah, right.

The bed-pod slid me into the tunnel. The earplugs barely blocked the loud whirring. I kept hearing "tumor…tumor… tumor" in rhythm to the MRI noises. Here I was, alone, strapped down with no control. No escape.

Think of something nice, something happy. The vision of Jason at the beach came to mind. Now as the machine roared around me, it instead chanted, "torso…torso…torso…" *Much better.*

"Hey there, you awake?" Troy's voice pierced through my torso-trance.

My eyes flew open, my skin a bit flushed.

"You're all set, trooper." Troy moved me out of the tunnel, undid the straps and helped me off the machine.

I clutched my gown tightly around me as I said, "Thank you," and climbed back into the wheelchair for my next carnival ride. *Whee.*

The bone scan and first CAT scan were quieter than the MRI. In preparation for the second CAT scan, another nurse injected me with a contrast solution. I had to wait for a few hours so the "nuclear medicine" (a serious oxymoron) could be fully absorbed into my bones. She explained the solution would create "hot spots" to highlight any diseased area of the bone. I somehow managed not to throw-up from her description.

She wheeled me back to the hospital room where Mom and I ate lunch and played gin with the cards Craig brought us, biding our time, trying not to think about my bones being momentarily nuclear and possibly *diseased*.

"Gin," I said as I put my last card down, and Mom groaned—it was my third win in a row. I bet she was purposely letting me win since I was not winning at real life today.

My phone rang. It was Dad.

"Ellie-bee. Are you okay? Your mom said they kept you overnight and you're getting scans?"

He hadn't called me Ellie-bee in years. It made me feel like I was ten again. "Hi, Dad. Are you coming to see me?" My voice sounded higher-pitched and needier than I meant, but I needed one of his bear hugs right now.

He coughed into the phone. A tic of his when he was uncomfortable. "Well…" He wasn't coming. "We just got to the airport. We're about to catch a flight to Maui for Barb's work conference and our vacation."

Oh right, Barb's *"We Can Do It"* conference, where she was getting an award for reaching a super special level of sales. Platinum, I think. Some sort of metallic recognition. I said nothing, wishing I hadn't asked if he was coming to the hospital.

He uncomfortable-coughed again. "Do you want me to cancel my flight?" He whispered the last part, clearly not wanting Barb to hear him say that.

Yes. Except I want you to just do it and not ask me. "No. It's okay. I have Mom here, and Craig."

And all my friends who seem to care so much more about me than you do.

Most of me wanted him to have a nice trip to Maui, just not the part that needed him to be here and hold me and call me his Ellie-bee.

We said our good-byes. I put my phone down and reached across the pile of cards and gave Mom a huge hug. She would have canceled her trip the second she knew I was in the hospital, even if it had been for some minor injury.

Breaking from the hug, I gathered up the cards and started shuffling them. Mom stared at me. "What, Mom?"

"Oh, you just have a *glow* about you." She laughed.

It took me a second to understand. "Mom, did you just make a joke about the radioactive tracer they put in me?"

She nodded, giggling some more. My mom's smile was the best.

When my last scan of the day was over, Darlene wheeled me back to the room. "You can change and head home now, dear. It will take a while to get the results from radiology."

"Thanks for your help today, Darlene."

"You bet, kiddo." She smiled and walked out.

As I changed out of the gown I studied my leg. It looked normal. Healthy. *They are being overly cautious. It's nothing.*

There was a knock, and Mom checked that I was fully clothed before she opened the door and someone stepped beside her.

"Jason?" I said, stupid with shock. I stuttered then managed to get out, "Mom, this is Jason Cooper. He does improv at Porter Township and had the party last night."

There was so much weirdness about this moment it was hard to keep it straight. What girl had to introduce her mom to the cute boy she'd just met? At a hospital? After getting scans for a tumor? I probably-not-so-covertly brushed my hand through my limp, greasy hair.

Mom shook his hand. "Hi, Jason. It is so kind of you to check in on Ellie."

"Hi. It's nice to meet you. And it's my policy to check on all house guests who are rushed off to the hospital in ambulances." He stuffed his hands in his pockets and gave a firm nod.

Mom stared at Jason oddly until the dry humor clicked. "Ah, yes, good policy." Her eyes flickered between us, and then she gathered up her stuff. "I'll just go make sure our release papers are in order and be back in a minute."

Jason thanked my mom and stepped further into the

room. "Sorry. Did I get here at a bad time?"

I just stared at him, jaw open, brain overloaded.

"Should I go? I should go, I just…did you get my text? I had to see you."

Had to. A smile bubbled up. "No, don't. Stay for a sec… if you can."

"So, are you okay?" He smiled, little creases forming around one side of his mouth, and I didn't know what to say or how to explain. I'd been given zero answers.

"Were you going to kiss me on the porch last night?" I blurted at him instead. *The radioactive tracer has made me bold.*

"I, uh, wasn't expecting that question." He stepped closer, a mock-serious look on his face. "The better question is, did you think I was going to kiss you and therefore throw yourself down a flight of stairs?"

I scoffed. "I can't believe it. I'm in the hospital and you're going to point out my lack of grace?"

He laughed. "For the record, I'm not calling you graceless. I'm asking about your flight response, because I might have gone over it a few times last night…" His voice got so quiet that I could just make out the rest of his sentence under his breath. "When I didn't sleep at all, thinking of you."

I internally and silently bounced and squealed. "Thinking about me?"

"Well, first, obviously, I wondered if you were okay, but once Quinn let me know you hadn't broken anything, I came up with the top five reasons you didn't want to kiss me."

I smiled too big, heat filling my face. Trying to act calm, I asked, "So? Reasons?"

He rubbed his forehead. "Well, if you want to go there, um, one: Maybe I had beastly breath and so you threw yourself off the deck to escape me."

"No. Your breath smelled like sugar and sunshine."

"Hmm, specific. Okay, two: I opened up about my mother and freaked you out. So, you chose to jump down a flight of stairs to get away before I mentioned cancer."

My blood cells collided to a stop. "No, that wasn't—wait, what do you mean cancer?"

"That's how Mom died. Stage four breast cancer." He took a deep breath. "This hospital reminds me of her, actually. It's where she was treated. Sorry. How are you? You never said what you're still doing here?"

"I…" I couldn't tell him the details. No way. Not now. Tumor, biopsy, those words would remind him of his mom. My brain scrambled. "I…" *I'll get the results back and find out it's nothing, and I won't have to bring any of it up.* "Nothing, really. They saw something on my bone in the X-rays that they needed to check out, and…anyway, I can go home now."

"Sorry, Ellie. If only I hadn't tried to kiss you, none of this would have happened."

"No, no, I'm the idiot who stepped *away* from the cute guy instead of *toward* him."

"Cute guy, eh? I'll take it." He gave me his irresistible side-smile again and took my hand in his.

"Uh, so what were you saying? Reasons? I believe you were on number three."

He looked up to the ceiling and then back at me. "My favorite reason: you were pretending to be pulse-stoppingly-pretty and hilarious and talented, with just enough weirdness to keep you interesting—but deep down you're a heartbreaker who likes to entice boys from other schools and then leap out of reach just when they think they can go in for the kiss."

"Excuse me? Heartbreaker?" *Pulse-stoppingly-pretty? He said pulse-stoppingly-pretty.*

"Four: you fell instantly in love with me but lost your courage, so you hurled yourself from great heights to get away."

"Whoa." I laughed, my stomach feeling like Harold the goldfish was in there doing his freak-out laps. "So, you really think I'm hilarious?"

"Out of all of that, that's what you take away?"

I shrug-nodded. Energy thrummed between our hands.

I couldn't resist asking, "What was the last reason?"

"Number five. The hard facts: you really didn't want to kiss me. But I can handle —"

"Definitely not it," I said softly.

"Definitely not?" he asked, looking happy.

"Definitely not."

"You know, it's a funny thing about this room we're in." He pointed all around me, as if this was crucial info. "There aren't any patios, stairways, or cliffs from which you could fling yourself right now."

"Huh." I examined the room as if this was real news. "Interesting. Should I call you Sherlock?"

"No. You should let me kiss you now."

He didn't make a move at first. He held my gaze in a way that made it impossible for me to think of any more words to say. It was just like our moment onstage together, when we could read each other wordlessly. But this time, no audience. I don't know who moved in closer first, him or me, or when, but there was definitely less space between us. His head leaned toward me, my chin tilted up. His other hand moved to gently touch my cheek as his lips finally, finally met mine. Gurneys and IV stands creaked and wheeled by outside the door. Names were announced over the intercom. Beeps emitted from medical monitors in some other room. It didn't matter. My whole body was light and bubbly. And his lips felt amazing, more amazing that anything I could have imagined.

Chapter Six

The members of Las Palomas del Disco, the working title of our sketch for the Comedy Hub contest, were sprawled around Craig's living room the Thursday night after Jason's party, tasked with our different assignments. I was ignoring texts and phone calls from Mom and plotting how I could get Jason away from everyone else so we could continue what we'd started in the hospital. There were also the star shapes I was tracing, of course, but ignoring and plotting were my *important* tasks.

Craig worked on his laptop and keyboard playing *Una Paloma Blanca* over and over again, its zippy snare beats and chirpy flutes filling the house. He'd found an instrumental version (karaoke saves the day) so he didn't have to recreate the whole track, but he was adding a few of his own layers, plus the random dove coos featured in the Spanish version we'd loved so much.

"Is it a bad sign I'm already sick of this sickly-sweet tune and it's only our first session?" Hana asked in that clipped way of hers.

"Maybe you could use some headphones, and *spare-us* the *snare-us*?" Owen suggested from his spot next to Quinn, organizing piles of gold spandex. We all groaned at the way he tried the spare/snare thing. I liked Owen, but he was punny.

"If Craig has to suffer, we all suffer together," Quinn said. "Anyway, I like the song. It makes me feel like I'm a butterfly flying around the Alps."

I stared at her, waiting for her to get it. "Or, say…a *dove*?"

"In *Spain*?" Jason added. He was cutting a star out of glitter paper next to me, and he had a particularly charming way of holding scissors.

A charming way of holding scissors? Maybe there is a tumor in my brain.

Quinn stopped her sewing machine, her face pensive. "No, I'm sticking with a butterfly in the Alps."

We all laughed.

"I *get* what you're all suggesting, I'm just saying, *that's* how it makes *me feel*. And I like it."

"Craig, I can't believe you live in a house by yourself. Is it awesome? Does your mom check on you a lot? How'd you pull that one off?" Owen asked.

Craig shrugged. "I told her there was no way I was moving to bumble Wisconsin my last year of high school. That I was already eighteen and supposed to go off to college next year anyway, so if she was going it was without me. She agreed."

"Sweet," Owen said.

"Yeah, she said she'd come home every weekend, but she rarely does. Now she just sends a grocery delivery service. So, it's the best of both worlds—all the food, none of the rules."

My heart broke a little for him, and for Jason, who was sitting next to me completely still, his head low. How cruel is the world that the good mom dies and the bad mom just voluntarily moves away?

"What do you mean *supposed* to go to college?" I asked.

"I want to do music. I'm doing music. Why start my life in debt when music is most likely never going to bring in enough cash to pay off student loans?"

I opened up my mouth to argue. I'd always been focused on college, and I still wasn't sure what I want to major in or do with my entire life. Craig was right—it didn't really make sense for him. I kind of envied his assuredness. *My world is officially upside down.*

Craig stopped the track. A second later, a different version of the same song started up, this one in English. "Owen, dude. This British guy from the seventies looks just like you." Craig pointed at his screen, and we all dropped what we were doing to gather around his laptop.

The singer doing the cover did look like Owen, with his reddish hair, thin face, and wire framed glasses.

"This one might be even cheesier than the first," Jason said.

"And why are they singing all the words in English, except *Una Paloma Blanca*, which they're saying with the most British accent possible?" Craig said. "It's ridiculous."

"Maybe we should do this version and Owen can be this British guy?" Quinn suggested.

We all paused and considered this.

I shook my head. "This version is funny, but no one will know that this guy looks like Owen so that will be lost on the audience. I've been thinking about it, and instead of trying to have one of the guys look and act just like the tall, debonair Spanish singer, we should have Hana dress in drag and be the lead."

"I like it," Owen said.

"I have just the thing." Quinn ran to the bin of props she'd brought and came back with a brown poufy man's wig. She put it on Hana, and we all reveled in the glorious sight.

Jason started nodding and slow clapping. "That's it."

Hana said, "I'm down. Short Korean girls like me never get to be the lead. This is why I love comedy. But what about, um, my ladies." She pointed to her ample chest. "They'll be hard to hide in a spandex jumpsuit."

Quinn pursed her lips. "I've got it. We stuff the rest of you to make you look either really muscular or really chubby."

We all shouted out our votes and were evenly split.

"Okay, TBD on that choice," Quinn said. "Or, maybe we'll have to do something entirely different with your costume, Hana." She got out her measuring tape.

Jason and I sat down and started tracing and cutting again.

"Do you think you and I should pause on the stars and work on choreographing the dance while we're all together?" Jason asked. "Since that will take time to memorize?"

"You have a point."

Dancing alone with Jason? Um, yes, please.

Dr. Nichols's warning about my leg popped into my mind. *I'll take it easy.*

Jason and I went into the kitchen and I set my phone up on the table so we could watch the video for ideas.

Pointing to the screen I said, "I think that's a good, easy way to start. All of us in a row doing low kicks to the side in unison." I demonstrated, mimicking the dancers in the video by overly gyrating my hips and shoulders as I stepped and kicked from side to side in time with the music.

Jason looked like he was trying to stifle a laugh. He had really nice lips. Really nice.

"Are you laughing at my mad dance skills?"

He shook his head with a playful grin, stepping closer to me. "I don't know how I'm going to focus on studying this choreography, when you're doing all that…uh, bouncing and wiggling."

I paused and bit my lower lip to try and stop from smiling. "This is serious, Jason Cooper." I gave him my best high-and-mighty tone. "Dance is an art form, and I like to win. Head in the game and do not let yourself get distracted."

He moved even closer. "Too late." We were only an inch apart.

How is it possible for someone to smell so good?

My phone pinged. My mother, the kiss-thwarter.

Jason widened his eyes at my phone. "Ellie, do you know you have seven missed texts from your mom?"

I didn't realize there'd gotten to be so many. I scrolled through them:

"Call me!"

"Did you see I called?"

"Call me back."

"It's important. I didn't want to text you this, but Dr. Nichols called. I need you to come home now."

"Ellie I've called three times. You're in big trouble."

"I'm on my way to get you."

My hand shook as I pocketed my phone. "Sorry, I have to go."

"Is everything okay?" Jason asked again as he followed me back into the living room.

"It'll be fine. She's mad I ignored her." I couldn't look at him.

I hate Dr. Nichols.

I gathered my backpack and art supplies as fast as I could. "Guys, I didn't realize it was so late. My mom's coming to pick me up. I'll finish the stars at home and plan out some more choreography that we can all rehearse next time." The heat of fear and shame spread across my cheeks.

"We should probably all get going. I can drive you," Quinn said.

"It's okay—" The doorbell rang. I sighed and opened the door. Mom stood before me fuming, her eyes red and blotchy like she'd been crying. I was a terrible daughter. *Why didn't I answer one of her calls?* "I'm sorry, Mom. I just saw all your texts a second ago. I—"

"Did you have dinner?"

"No, why?"

This is the big concern?

Mom peered over me, ignoring my question. "Hi, Craig. Hi, kids. We have to go, but please check in with your parents every once in a while. They'll appreciate it. Craig, let me know if you need anything, okay, honey?"

"I'm good, thanks, Sonia."

I started down the steps. "Why do you care so much if I had dinner?"

"Ellie, Dr. Nichols had a cancelation and moved up your biopsy for first thing in the morning. You can't eat for twelve hours before, and now it's too late to eat. I didn't want you to be hungry in the morning." Her voice was terse yet tired.

I glanced behind me and saw Jason's stricken face right before the door closed. He'd heard what Mom said. They probably all did.

We got in the car and both slammed our doors. "Why'd she schedule my biopsy so last-minute? What are they going to do to me that I can't eat for twelve hours beforehand?"

She let out a puff of pissed-off air. "Well, that's what I've been trying all night to communicate with you, Ellie. You know you have to at least check in with me when you're out of the house. It's my one rule. Especially when we're dealing with all this, I expect you to over-communicate with me from now on. Keep your phone on, by your side, and answer all of my calls and texts immediately."

She never freaked out on me like this. "Mom. What is going on? What did Dr. Nichols say?"

Mom gripped the wheel like she might tear it off, and steadied her voice. "She...she had a last-minute opening so they were able to get you in sooner." She didn't look at me.

"You can't eat because they're going to cut through your leg to get to your bone, and you will have to be put under for that."

My whole body tensed and one whimper escaped. For some reason, I'd imagined they'd stick a long needle into my leg like drawing blood, which was scary enough. "I didn't know I'd be knocked out and cut open," I whispered. I didn't want to do this. I couldn't do this.

"Oh sweetie. I'm so sorry." Mom turned and hugged me to her. I buried my face in her hair and squeezed my eyes shut as tight as I possibly could.

Chapter Seven

The morning of the biopsy I waited with Mom in another hospital room, in another green gown, my stomach growling with the vengeance of a thousand told-you-sos. My phone pinged with a text from Jason. It was a cute picture of puppies. What else do you do when someone's getting a biopsy? I'd texted with everyone last night, because of course they all overheard Mom tell me about the biopsy on the stairs and were worried about me. Which was super great.

Jason was kind, but what did he really think? He lost his mom a little over a year ago. Now the first girl he's kissed since then has a tumor? It was messed up.

A nurse came in and handed Mom a big plastic bag with my patient ID number on it. "This is for Ellie's belongings. She'll be in post-op after surgery and then released, so you two won't be coming back to this room."

The nurse had me climb onto the gurney and stuck an IV in my arm. *Ouch.* The pricked spot stung as the nurse wheeled me down the cold halls away from my mom. I caught glimpses into other surgery rooms with bright lights and huddles of masked faces as I prayed I'd be okay and drifted away.

Waking up, I fought to resurface from the pool of pudding where someone must have tried to drown me. Muscles heavy, breathing tight, brain unfocused. I didn't know if I was making noise, but a young nurse came over with a cup of ice chips. She encouraged me to open my mouth, and slipped in an ice-chip. It cooled my dry mouth. *So thirsty.* As if reading my thoughts, she told me I wasn't allowed water yet. Tubes poked out of me, and the nurse pointed out the button I could press to ease the pain. *Isn't that nice—relief at the press of a button?*

If only all of life were that simple—a morphine-drip for the soul. The drugs oozed into my veins, knocking me out again.

The next time I woke up, Mom was there. She smiled. I tried to smile. Out again.

In and out of consciousness for I don't know how long. Amid the fog of nurses, machines, beeping, the first inkling of pain in my leg, a scratchy throat, moans that didn't belong to me, maybe some that did, I picked up a few bits of information. The biopsy had gone well, I shouldn't get my leg wet for three days, and I could go home. I didn't have to spend the night at the hospital.

Eventually I was disconnected from my IV and morphine drip, cumbersomely helped into a wheelchair, and pushed to the juice-and-graham-cracker room. Another hour-long wait. You could track the movement of the minute hand on the clock by Mom's repetitive sighing.

Then my leg woke up. It was cranky, demanding morphine. The chair I sat in became its own little torture device, where the slightest shift was like an icepick to my thigh.

Pain. I'd been asked my level of pain—a scale from one

to ten, like that meant anything to me—a bunch since this thing started. What's the point of rating things that can't really be rated? The stabby-throbbing didn't have a number—it just hurt a lot—so I'd answer: *I don't know, between five and six?* Not knowing if this made me a drama queen or someone to ignore.

I chewed on the cuticle of my thumb.

Why is this happening? Did I do something wrong?

"Is it my fault this thing is inside me?" I hadn't meant it to, but the last thought came out as a whisper. *Crap.*

"Oh sweetie, no, no, of course not." Mom took my hand and squeezed it, giving me a sad smile and pensive eyes. "I never told you this part of your birth story, but…"

Okay, random. "Um, are you saying being pregnant is like having a tumor inside you?"

She screwed up her face into shock, and let out one big belly laugh. "What? For goodness' sake, no. What I was *going* to say is that I worked to do everything right for your birth. I ate healthy, drank lots of water, took us on walks, and told us peaceful, encouraging thoughts."

I smiled. I'd heard this, but I liked the thought of her taking her belly—with me inside—on walks.

"You know the part where I tried so hard to not have any medication during your birth."

"But then you needed an emergency C-section."

"That's right. You kept springing back up every time I pushed, and they were worried about your heart. But the part I left out is that I screamed and wailed down that hall into surgery, like a wild animal torn out of her nest."

Whoa. This surprised me.

She put her other hand on top of our clasped hands.

"I felt like a failure, like my first act as a mom had failed you. The nurse came back and put you on my chest and said to me, 'you did great, you did your best. All that matters in all of this is that little peanut in your arms.' And she was right."

She kissed my forehead. "I'm so grateful for you, baby girl. The point of my story is that I know a little of what it feels like to have your body not cooperate with your hopes. That we have to keep focused on what's important, which is to make sure you're healthy. Right? Mostly I'm saying, *it's not your fault.*"

My lips trembled.

Nurse Darlene came to check on me and examined my chart. "It looks like you'll need some crutches, so I've scheduled you a session with a physical therapist for training."

"What? What do you mean she'll need crutches? No one told us that," Mom said.

Darlene's chin squished into her neck. She had no idea and bustled off to find someone who did. Didn't they know I had improv and sketch rehearsals? Our second show at the Comedy Mash-Up a week from today?

Mom clutched my hand, saying, "It'll be okay, sweetie, it'll be okay."

The nurse came back after a while and explained that I could be on crutches anywhere from two weeks to a month.

"A *month*?" Mom stood up, outraged for both of us. "And no one considered this important information? We were told this was a simple procedure."

"I'm sorry no one mentioned it to you, Mrs. Hartwood. The procedure was relatively simple but the incision went through her muscles and into the bone right above her knee. This will cause weakness, and she'll need support."

Mom's jaw set in the way it does when she's furious. Her hand gripped mine tighter.

I went still and silent.

It didn't sound like I'd be in any condition to dance disco.

The physical therapist arrived. I hated the sight of the silver metal in her arms.

She slipped the padded tops under my armpits, and I gripped the two rubbery handles, having to round my shoulders slightly. Standing firmly on my right leg, I swung both crutches forward until the stoppers hit the linoleum floor. *Ka-clunk.*

"Good," she said, so upbeat. "That's it, Ellie. You got it."

Ka-clunk. Ka-clunk. The *Transformers* theme song started playing in my head. Great. It would be *Una Paloma Blanca* versus *Transformers* battling it out for worst sticky song in my brain for the next month.

As I practiced, I could hear Mom and Dr. Nichols talking.

"When will we learn the results of the biopsy?" Mom was in don't-mess-with-me mode.

"The labs often take longer with bone tissue," Dr. Nichols said. "We can expect to know in seven to ten days. We'll call to schedule an appointment when we have the results."

My lungs squeezed. My grip tightened. Why didn't the doctor say something reassuring?

Swallowing hard, I glared at her, even though she couldn't see me. *Please tell me she is just being dramatic. Please.*

Mom returned, and we were released with a bag of drugs, two crutches, one swollen leg (and a partridge in a pear tree).

Chapter Eight

The Vicodin didn't like me. I spent the entire night and morning after surgery throwing up every hour. Nothing like having your mom wipe vomit off your face and dress you to make you feel mature and ready to be an adult.

College, here I come.

The slightest movement caused a deep ache in my thigh. Who knew an inch slice from skin to bone could cause so much trouble? As soon as the doctor's office opened on Saturday, Mom ran out to get a different painkiller prescription and medicine to ease my nausea, plus she promised to bring back ginger ale and animal crackers. Before she left, she set me up on the floor with cushions, a stack of books, and the remote at the ready. Moms are the best.

Jason called one of the times I was in the bathroom. Even in my hideous state, his voicemail caused a brief moment of excitement. "Hey, Ellie. You're probably resting. How'd it go? Hope you're healing up."

He was so sweet, and I missed his voice. But what if I called him and had to throw up mid-sentence? That would not be romantic.

I texted.

Everything is fine. Except on crutches for a few weeks. Tragic. Pain meds making me feel kinda ick. But let's talk soon.

And then I immediately threw up again. *Sexxxxy.*

At six p.m. on the Monday after my biopsy, I woke from a second nap to my phone vibrating. It was hard to believe it had only been nine days since Jason's party. I carefully shifted to sitting up on my raft of cushions on the living room floor, where'd I'd spent the day elevating my still-swollen leg, doing homework and watching romantic comedies.

There was a text from Quinn:

Finished Spontaneous Combustion practice. Wasn't right without you. XOXO.

I'd missed a text from Hana a couple hours ago, too.

How am I supposed to co-captain without my co? This is a bucket of turds, I tell you.

I laughed, and then cried. Hana was kidding, but I should be there, helping the newbies, supporting my team. And what about our sketch for the contest? How would I rehearse? I prayed that it would be benign. It *had* to be.

I'm healthy and seventeen.

"Aw hell, no, sis. Don't start crying on me when I'm on babysitting duty."

"Craig? *Jesus.*" I practically jumped off the cushions, which caused a huge jolt of pain in my leg, telling me it was time for another dose of the new painkillers. I wiped at my eyes and pulled my blanket higher, wishing I could hide under it completely. Craig stood there in sweatpants and no shirt.

"I get that comparison a lot, but you're too kind." Craig shrugged.

"What?"

"How much I'm like Jesus. Is it the hair? Time for a cut?" He swished his longish hair back and forth.

"When did you get here? And why don't you have a shirt on?"

"Because it's hotter than Satan's balls in here."

"I was cold. Bring me another blanket and you can crack the slider. Where's Mom?"

He threw a blanket at me, and walked over to open the sliding-glass door. "Fresh air. I thought I'd never breathe you again." He stuck his head out the window and inhaled exaggeratedly. "Your mom's picking up Thai food, should be home in a minute. I'm your knight in zero armor."

My stomach growled in response, knowing she was getting my favorite post-sick meal of coconut lemongrass soup.

Craig slid the door closed all but a sliver and walked over to adjust the thermostat. "Want to watch some *Ranma*? I witnessed your collection of movies, and I have to tell you, that line of DumbCom is not going to continue while I'm here."

"Okaaay—maybe, what's a 'Ranma?'"

"Ridiculous Japanese Anime from the nineties."

"Oddly, I *do* want to watch that. Must be the drugs messing with my mind. But you have to put on a shirt."

"There's a reason God gifted me with great muscles, babe. You don't want to cover up God's gift." He gave me a flex show.

And with that, the pity-fest faded into the background of my mind. "Yes. Yes, I do. Now, go put on some clothes."

He nodded, grabbing his T-shirt. It was weird how in the

last three years we'd orbited around the same giant school, in the same grade with six hundred other students, but never been in the same classes. Craig, perpetually huddled in the music hall being all musicy, and me, always backstage or onstage doing my theater thing, our lives never intertwining, until—*bam*—our parents fell in love and got married, pairing us up as brother and sister.

At first, I blamed him for all that was wrong with my parents. But it was my dad who screwed up. I'd never wanted a brother before, but right now I felt lucky.

By the time Mom got home, Craig had laid out a second sea of pillows and blankets for himself next to mine. *Ranma* was paused and ready to play.

"What's this?" Mom asked.

"Japanese anime. Want to join us, Mom?"

Mom glanced at the image of a cartoon boy and panda on the screen, flared her nostrils and bugged her eyes. "Too bizarre for me. I'm glad to see a smile back on your face, so I think I'll go watch some normal TV in my room. Love you, sweetie. Thank you for coming over and helping out, Craig." She kissed us both on our heads, took her meal out of the bag and left us the rest.

Craig pressed play.

"Whoa. Giant karate-chopping pandas? I think I'm going to love this."

Craig nodded, his cheeks full of pad thai.

I gulped down the soup and rice as we watched the magic of *Ranma* unfold before us. At the end of the first episode, I announced with a pout, "I'm still hungry."

"Well, as it turns out, I'm competing for best stepbrother of the year, and knowing the pathetic state of your snack cabinet, I came prepared."

Craig headed to the kitchen. When he returned, he threw me a bag of cereal labeled Marshmallow Mateys, which were exactly like Lucky Charms, but more generic and with treasure-themed marshmallows instead of charms. Also, packaged in a gigantic bag. *Score.*

"Hey." I held up the bag of cereal dramatically. "Is *this* what you mean when you always say 'eat a bag'?"

"Yes, yes, Ellie, that is exactly what I mean. Also, you're hilarious."

"I know. Right? It's my special skill." I gave a toothy grin as he handed me two cereal bowls. "Yeah, those aren't going to cut it. Could you grab the green and orange mixing bowls, pleeease?"

He made a face like he was impressed. "I truly appreciate a woman who isn't going to pretend we're not about to stuff our faces."

"Yep."

When he settled back in, I poured cereal and milk into the two gigantic mixing bowls he'd grabbed for us, and he pressed play.

Between drippy mouthfuls, I asked questions. "So, like, what's with the water changing them? Why does Ranma turn into a girl, and the father into a Panda?"

"Because of the cursed springs."

I raised an eyebrow. He pressed pause and turned to look at me seriously.

"See, when someone falls into a cursed spring, they take the physical form of whatever drowned there years ago. So, Ranma fell into the Spring of the Drowned Girl, so he turns into a girl. And his dad fell into the Spring of the Drowned Panda."

"Sure, of course."

He pressed play.

By the end of the third episode, my body fought with itself: the sugar crash making my eyelids droopy, but everything else in me wanting to keep watching and laughing.

"Do you want to sleep, or are you up for another?" Craig asked, holding up the remote.

"Press play, and we'll see what happens."

"Can we take bets?"

"Absolutely not." Episode four began, and I gave in to the sleepiness, sinking lower onto the floor, adjusting the pillow under my head and pulling the blankets up to my chin. When my eyes fluttered open again, Craig was still awake. He was sitting upright and laughing.

"Craig?" I was trying so hard to get my eyelids to open all the way.

"Yeah?"

"Do you ever think about your dad?"

"My dad? Dude, go for the jugular much?"

"Sorry, never mind."

"No, it's okay. I used to. I asked Mom about him when I was younger. But now I don't. There's no point. He was a one-night stand, and she never even knew his last name. Only that he was, in her words, 'A tall, dark, handsome, guitar-playing heartbreaker.'"

I shuddered. "Bet you were sorry you even asked."

"Big time."

"Are you mad at Barb and my dad for leaving you here all alone?"

Craig didn't answer.

"Tell me."

"Shh, go to sleep, Ellie."

I tried to rally myself and sat up a bit more. "You can tell me. Is it lonely?"

"Nah. I can stay up as late as I want and eat Marshmallow Mateys for every meal." He held up his empty bowl and grinned too big.

"Yeah, right." I don't know if it was the sleepiness factor or what, but I snuggled up against him, and he put his arm gently around me.

"It must be lonely," I said as I fell asleep, thankful that while we were both down a parent, we at least had each other.

After I'd spent another painkiller-hazy day at home, Craig came over again in the evening with more Marshmallow Mateys and *Ranma.*

Hero.

A few episodes in, the throbbing in my leg kicked back in so I took another pill and fell asleep on our raft of cushions. A little after eight p.m., Craig stirred, and I opened my eyes to see him getting up.

"Where're you going?"

"If you must know, I'm going to drop a deuce."

"Gross."

"You asked." He strutted away and a minute later our intercom buzzed.

Mom shuffled to the buzzer, confirmed it was Hana and Quinn, and pressed the button to let in my friends.

I brushed back my hair, hoping I didn't look like a murder of crows had attacked me.

Mom opened the door to our apartment, and Quinn and Hana came in, followed by Jason.

I'd have to kill my best friends for not warning me.

"Hey, Ellie," they chirped.

"Hi," I said with my best cheery grin.

Mom said her hellos and went back to her room.

"I can't shower, and I'm on drugs. Fair warning. How was sketch rehearsal?"

They formed a semi-circle around me in our cramped living room.

"It was…okay," Quinn said, clearly not wanting me to

feel like I'd missed too much, but too bad, I already did.

"We were definitely missing a backup dove," Jason said. "These are for you." He handed me a mason jar with three paperboard flowers painted with bright swirls of color.

"These are so beautiful. Did you make them?" He nodded shyly. "Wow, improv, singing, and painting? A real Renaissance man."

He gave me a somber smile. "My mom used to say that."

"Oh, I'm sorry, I—"

"No," he stopped me. "It's okay, I like hearing it."

Talking to someone who'd lost a parent was like a word minefield. It had to be hard for him—there must be something every day that reminded him of her. Not that he'd want to forget her, it just seemed that kind of grief must always be in reach, a constant shadow.

Quinn ran to where they had dropped their stuff by the front door, and then walked backward toward me until she got to my sea of cushions and turned around to reveal a fishbowl in her hands. "Ta da!"

"Aw, thanks, you guys." I could've hugged the bowl. I don't know why seeing Harold comforted me, but it did.

Hana handed me a small box. "This is from Quinn and me."

"Open it," Quinn demanded.

I unwrapped the box and lifted off the lid. Inside was a silver necklace with a pendant shaped like a bull's head, its eyes made of tiny green jewels. "I love it, thank you. You two really shouldn't have. Why a bull's head?"

"For one, we know you're all into Colorado and the West and we couldn't find a pendant of horses or mountains last minute, and figured there're probably bulls there, too," Hana said.

Quinn took the necklace and clasped it around my neck. "*More importantly*, the bull stands for cosmic order and strength. Things you could use in life, no matter what this turns out to be."

I liked the feel of the cool silver and the weight of the pendant against my chest. It did seem like it could bring strength and cosmic goodness.

"It also stands for stubbornness and male virility, but we chose to focus on the other stuff," Hana added.

I laughed. "It's perfect."

They gave me the play-by-play of rehearsal, which included Hana reenacting the dove flying choreography they decided on. She loped around our living room and flapped her arms.

"No. You're forgetting. We decided on this move," Quinn protested, flapping her arms with an exaggerated shoulder roll. "And this part." She did a funny shimmy-kick with her feet and bobbled her head every time she moved.

"Oh, you're right." Hana flapped again and added the little kick and headshake. Now there were two arm-flapping, head-waggling birds hopping around the living room making the most obnoxious noises. Jason stood with his hands in his pockets, a stiff smile on his face. *What is he thinking?*

Mom came out of her room, looking bewildered at Hana and Quinn.

"You two are too much." She laughed until she glanced at me and stopped, her expression changing as if she could see I was getting tired. "Thank you, our dear court jesters, for coming over, but I think the queen needs her rest now."

"C'mon, Mrs. Hartwood, get your dancin' disco dove on," Hana said, putting her hands under her armpits and flapping right over to Mom. Mom was considering it, a glimmer of a smile on her face. Hana had that effect on parents, having some sixth sense of how to push them enough to budge, but not so far they would get all parental.

Mom paused for a second and then said, "Well, okay," as

she started lunging around the room, waving her arms and doing some odd elbow-jerk thing all her own. I hated to not be part of the game, but I loved having my friends come over and laughing together. Even if they were making so much noise I was sure the neighbors would knock and complain.

Jason sat next to me on the floor. "It looks even better with the music."

I tilted my head, doubtful. "That's the beauty of comedy. Even if it doesn't look good, it still works."

He gave a weak laugh. "Yeah." He scraped at nothing on the knee of his jeans. "So, you had a biopsy?"

My chest deflated. *Oh God.* I sucked in air, scrambling for an explanation that didn't sound pathetic. "I'm sorry I didn't tell you I had to get a biopsy, that I said it was nothing. I still think it will be nothing, but until then, it's obviously kinda something. Anyway, they're being overly cautious. Doctors."

He clamped his lips and nodded, his focus still on anything but me. "I get it...I—"

Not sure if it was how badly this conversation was going, or all the spinning and jumping happening around us, or the medication, but I didn't hear the rest of his sentence because the room swayed.

Mom immediately stopped her shenanigans. The others got the hint too and—*poof*—no more disco doves.

"Ellie, are you okay?" Jason steadied me by the shoulders and handed me my glass of water. I took a sip and a deep breath. "Thank you." The room evened out, but the loopiness ramped up a notch.

There was a flush from down the hall and everyone turned to watch Craig walk out of the bathroom. "I don't know what was going on out here while I was laying some pipe, but I feel like I should either clap or bow." He bowed.

"Gross." I stuck out my tongue. I took another sip of water and tried to keep my eyelids from drooping.

"Hi, Craig," Hana said. Her eyes bugged out at his bare chest.

Without meaning to, I laughed and said, "Hana, your face. You got it bad." Then I clapped a hand over my mouth.

Hana shot me death glares.

I scrambled to get up on my crutches and try to stand, which was painful and awkward and slow and not worth it. Jason stood with me, arms at the ready like he might have to catch me, which wasn't a bad idea. When I finally got my balance, I said, "Hana, I…I'm sorry, it just came out."

"What?" Craig asked. "What's she got b—?" Then he looked at Hana, realization dawning.

"I gotta go." Hana fled our apartment.

When the door shut behind her, Craig stammered then said, "Should I go after her?" He paused for a moment. "Yeah, I'm gonna go talk to her."

He put his shirt on and left, the door slamming for a second time.

Quinn hugged me close, as close as she could around two crutches. "It's okay, I'll talk to her. We shouldn't have surprised you like this." Quinn headed out, too. *Slam. Can't anyone gently close the door as they run away from my horrible company?*

Now I was even more embarrassed about my mental and hygienic state as I faced Jason, who was playing the part of a mannequin with his eyes wide and arms stiff by his sides.

"Sorry for all that," I said. "And I'm sorry again about not telling you everything earlier."

Shut up.

"Seriously, I get it. Don't worry about it. I'm really sorry you're going through all this. Can I help? My family has made a lot of connections since…" He trailed off.

"No, no. Thank you. Like I said, they're just being annoyingly thorough. I'll be fine."

He nodded. "Of course, yeah. Well, I'll call you, okay? I should get going, too." He gave a wave of his hand and moved to leave, as I stepped forward like we were going to hug. We did this shuffle hug that was all elbows and crutches and obligation.

That was the triple threat of terrible.

The door shut behind him. A punch of silence. Mom patted my shoulder as I hobbled past her to my room. I threw the crutches on the floor and flopped on the bed, my head spinning with painkillers, ways to apologize to Hana, and tremors of panic that I'd scared Jason away forever.

Chapter Nine

The next day my leg still hurt, but I had to get to school to apologize to Hana in person. And also, you know, not get hopelessly behind in my classes. I searched Mom's closet to find something that would fit over my swollen leg, and grabbed a pair of baggy cargo pants.

My crutches made my normal getting-to-school routine exponentially longer. No one would suspect the decades it took to brush one's teeth and make a lunch when one was essentially a human set of tongs.

Late to school, I missed catching Hana backstage and went straight to my first class, which was alternative gym—yoga—this quarter. I started getting out my books, assuming Mrs. Lahiri would let me spend class in the back catching up on homework, since I could barely walk, let alone do yoga.

When Mrs. Lahiri saw me, she smiled wide and said, "Ellie, it is so good to see you." She instructed the class to continue with their sun salutations and squatted next to my mat. "How are you feeling?" I brightened a little. She was like an angel on earth or something—something beyond us mortals, at least.

"Not so good. It hurts when I try to bend my leg."

"Ellie, give yourself a break. Let me see." She had me sit on a chair and roll up my cargo pants so she could see the site of the biopsy, right above my left knee.

"It's better, but it still doesn't want to bend much."

"Do you stretch it to the edge of your pain?" She looked at me quizzically with her big almond eyes. I didn't know which answer was right.

"I thought it was bad to push it too far—I didn't want to make it hurt more."

She gazed out the windows of the gym to the parking lot and didn't say anything for a while. Finally, she turned to me. "Yes and no. As with all things in life, you must find the balance. Even though bending it to the edge of pain seems to cause more discomfort in the moment, after it is over, your body feels a release. Like in yoga with those twists I make you hold longer than you want—once you start focusing on your breath instead of the intensity of the stretch—"

"It gets easier, and then everything opens up," I finished.

She nodded. "Pain is sacred. It can be our greatest teacher and our greatest protector. That is why you must respect it and listen to it so closely."

I chewed my lower lip, not sure about this pain theory.

She took another stare-out-the-window pause. Did everyone who'd found inner peace do everything so slowly? If so, it wasn't the path for me.

"Most people are so scared of the pain in their life, they do anything they can to avoid it, to not feel what is really there. Ignoring it merely causes a different kind of hurt."

My skin went goose-bumpy. It seemed like she wasn't just talking about my leg anymore...but why?

For the rest of class, she led everyone else through the regular sequences and had me on the yoga mat doing "restorative" poses, which were kind of like napping while in an easy stretch. I couldn't get settled. I lay on my back, eyes wide open, biting down hard on the inside of my cheeks, waiting for the bell to ring, realizing I sucked at "letting go" and "going with the flow."

There's a lesson for you: don't do yoga.

You'll find crap out about yourself you don't want to know.

Crutching through the halls between classes, I caught snippets of conversation. It was only mid-September, but everyone was talking about homecoming next month. I'd forgotten about it.

By midday my body was done. Arms aching. Left leg swollen. Right leg wobbly from doing all the walking. And none of Mrs. Lahiri's advice to breathe deep or make pain my BFF was working.

"Hey, Ellie." It was Annabelle, a girl that used to live down the street before we moved. She put down her phone for a second. "Crutches are the worst. You okay?"

"Yeah, I'll be fine. Thanks." I repeated almost the same exchange with four more people, keeping up a smile that might as well have been plastic.

Fine, fine, fine. When, really, I had no idea what I was.

Their best sympathy faces sucked—like they knew they were supposed to express something, but didn't know how to actually feel it. I was doing the same thing. At least they were looking up from their phones and saying "hey" and trying. That was nice.

Instead of going to Statistics, I stepped into the bathroom, making sure I was alone, and maneuvered into the last stall.

I stared at the toilet seat, exhausted, debating. *Gross.* But the two darts lodged in my shoulders throbbed again so I sat down.

I could just burn these pants.

I shook out my arms and leg.

I let out a long sigh, needing a second to rally myself.

Buzz, buzz, buzz.

A fly was in the stall with me. It was shockingly loud for being such a tiny insect, its two wings like furious little chainsaws.

"Agh!" I pounded my fists against the bathroom wall.

The clamp around my lungs tightened.

Some weird muscle in my chest near my heart clenched.

Buzz, buzz.

That fly had to be destroyed. My fingers splayed and shook. I pounded my fist harder against the stall wall.

Buzz.

I gulped air, forgetting how to breathe.

Breathe, just breathe. It's okay, it's nothing, it's going to be nothing. You'll be okay.

Buzz.

Finally, I put all my focus on pulling air into my nostrils, long and slow, cooling them.

Buzz.

Breathe.

Buzz.

Breathe.

I found a rhythm with the fly.

The tears poured down my cheeks. *Air in, air out.* Again and again.

It'll be okay. It'll be okay. It'll be okay. It'll be okay. It'll be okay. It'll be okay.

Chapter Ten

The next day I woke up determined to stop with the pain meds and get to school early so I could make sure to find Hana. She was backstage with Quinn where we usually met up before class. Quinn was gathering her backpack, and Hana was stacking a can on her can pyramid by the stage door.

"Hana, I'm so incredibly sorry about the other night. Can you please forgive me? There's no excuse, but I was so—"

Hana gave me a Jedi wave to make me stop talking. "Didn't you get my email?"

"Email? Since when do you email me?"

"Since I acted like a baby and stormed out on you. And since your stepbrother asked me on a date. I needed to write all the best words, which I now see was a huge waste of time. Figures."

Relief. Plus, a lumpy mix of confusion. "So, you and Craig went on date? You're dating? Are you boyfriend and girlfriend? Did you make out?"

"Hold up. No to all the above. I was asked on a date, for tomorrow, after our second show at the Mash-Up. The rest, we shall see. Really, you should ask Quinn about her news."

Quinn clicked her tongue and gave Hana a shove.

"What is it? I want to know."

"I was going to tell you when we were at your apartment before everything got chaotic, but Owen asked me out after sketch rehearsal, and I said yes." She did the clappy-hands she did when she was excited. "He's about the funniest guy I've met, I mean, except for the puns, and he's so goofy and blunt and cute and—"

"What? Are you two kidding me?" I went to throw my arms up in the air, but since they were attached to metal, they kind of flopped to the side like lazy albatross wings as I balanced on one foot. "Are you four going on a double date?"

Quinn said, "Oh, weird, no," as Hana stared at me like that was the worst idea in the history of humankind.

I plopped down on the couch, adjusting to these epic, overnight changes. "What is going on? Don't get me wrong, I'm super happy for you both and want every detail. I'm just kind of shocked. I mean, is Cupid on a rampage?"

Quinn twisted her lips and narrowed her eyes. "When you put it that way, it does sound crazy. But let's not kid ourselves about why we all decided to form the sketch group together. I mean, it's not like Las Palomas del Disco is high art. It's fun, sure, but mostly an excuse, don't you think? To hangout? And you're the one who has already kissed Jason."

"Once." I let out an exasperated breath. "And after Tuesday night, I'm pretty sure he'll never want anything to do with me again."

I waited. They both stared at me, their mouths turning to unhelpful lines.

"Uh, why aren't you two reassuring me that I wasn't a deranged and frightening beast, and that any boy who had just lost his mom to cancer would jump at the chance to get involved with a girl on crutches boasting a suspicious tumor and an unknown future?"

Blinking eyes. Unhelpful mouth lines.

My phone pinged. "It's Jason," I announced, like it was a victory, and they let out sighs of relief that made me even more annoyed with them…and my life.

Jason: *Important question…*

I sat up, full alert.

Me: *Okay…*

Jason: *You're still coming to the Mash-Up, right?*

All the exhales.

Me: *I think no…kind of hard to do improv on crutches.*

Jason: *But I haven't given anyone a piggyback on stage in so long.*

I laughed thinking about the last show.

"Yo, Ellie, bated breath over here—what's he saying?" Hana asked.

"He's asking if I'm still going to perform in the show tomorrow."

"On crutches?" Quinn crinkled her nose.

"It'd be insane. But it's a good sign he's asking, right?"

"Right," they answered in unison.

Me: *Hmm…tempting. But I'm gonna go with crutches = no improv for me.*

Jason: *Nonsense. Crutches = automatic props.*

My smile spread. The second bell rang. "You two should head to class. I'm going to be late, but I have an excuse." I motioned my head to my crutches.

"We could make the improvising on crutches work. You should do it," Quinn said.

"I vote for it for the spectacle alone," Hana said as the two walked out to the bustle of the hallway.

I waved bye, focused back on my phone and typed,

Dynamics of crutch-prov... Go.

Crutch-prov. Nice.

Different rules?

Same commandments of improv, plus a bonus: Thou shalt not bludgeon thy scene partner with a crutch.

:) Or, thou shalt not use thy crutch to force thy scene partner to do the limbo.

Never. :)

We riffed back and forth before we typed our good-byes, and my corset of worry loosened.

Chapter Eleven

I stood backstage at Porter Township High School and listened to murmurs of the audience fill the theater. Unhooking the loop of the large water bottle lid from between my middle finger and crutch handle, I gently set Harold on the table, though the water still sloshed back and forth. I undid the lid to give him air again. "Sorry for the whirlpool adventure, lil' guy. Maybe I should have skipped my new policy about you for this show."

It had only been two weeks since our first show here, but — *look at me* — so much had changed. A wave of weepiness consumed me. Why had I agreed to this?

Scared Scriptless had asked Spontaneous Combustion if we wouldn't mind sticking to the short-form, game style we'd done at the first show, since they did long form and it gave the audience a nice mix. We agreed, and this time they started off the show.

I mostly fixated on Jason, the perfect distraction to get over myself. When he was on the sidelines, his eyes darted around, taking everything in. He kind of bounced on the balls of his feet with his arms crossed, ready to pounce in for a scene edit at any second. When he was onstage, I focused on the way his thigh muscles moved under his jeans, how his shoulder and chest muscles slid under his Scared Scriptless T-shirt as he morphed from regular Jason to his different characters—douchebag CEO, crass old Scottish man, sober pirate who found plundering distasteful. How his thick brown hair had a life of its own. How his lips moved when he spoke, begging to be kissed.

Between sets, Owen announced the contest again and shouted, "There are a few spots left in the contest lineup, so there is still time, folks. Don't hold back. *Commit.* The prizes? Five hundred dollars and your performance featured on Comedy Hub dot com." He continued bounding around the stage, his lanky limbs reminding me of those inflatable dancing tube men outside car dealerships.

When our set started, I lay low for the first few scenes, trying to get Jason out of my head so I could focus on how I was going to work this improv thing out on crutches.

Then came the game Forward/Reverse. Quinn started the scene with two others and Hana "called" it, which meant whenever she shouted "reverse," the actors would have to go backward through their action and dialogue to the beginning, or until Hana called "forward" again. Like forwarding or reversing a movie. This scene was about medieval knights who had to compete in a joust.

I was enjoying watching from the sidelines when Chris, the ex-football-player in our group, appeared next to me pushing an office chair he must have found backstage. He raised his eyebrows as if to say, "Ya in?" I immediately knew his plan and, putting one crutch down, I sat in the chair and propped the other crutch out parallel to the floor. Within seconds both of us were yelling, "Charge!" as Chris wheeled me, the jousting knight, quickly across the stage. The audience went nuts for our prop-comedy, clapping and shouting. New electric energy fueled me. After that, I jumped into scene after scene, eventually having to hold myself back so I wouldn't hog the stage.

After the show, Craig came up and gave me such a big hug he lifted me and the crutches off the floor for a second. "Impressive, sis. I was sure I would hate it, but it turns out improv is kinda cool. It's like the jazz of theater, huh?"

"Yeah, I guess so. Thanks." I smiled, realizing Craig's approval now meant something to me.

"This is my friend Luke, and you guys totally blew his mind," Craig said, gesturing to his college-aged friend. He was a scrawny guy with black hair and elaborate piercings and tattoos. Apparently, Luke wasn't much for words, but he mimed his mind exploding and made a bomb-like sound effect.

Hana came up, and Craig leaned down to hug her, too, in a long, lingering way. "You are a queen of comedy." She blushed.

Then Scared Scriptless's group gathered in with ours, and I was face-to-face with Jason. He was about to say something, when Mom came over to us, along with a handsome man in his forties or fifties.

"Hi, Dad," Jason said to the man next to my mom.

"Hi, Ellie. I'm Jason's dad, Michael." He smiled, and I could immediately see the similarities. "I've heard so much about you and it's nice to see all that talent in action. The joust scene was my favorite. Very creative use of crutches." He patted me on the shoulder.

I managed to say, "Thank you. So nice to meet you," and resisted saying: I'm so sorry about your wife. Your son is one of my favorite humans on earth. Why have you heard about me? How did you meet my mother?

"Jason has told me a little of what you're going through,

and I want to say, we are here for you if you need anything. Anything at all," Mr. Cooper said. Jason came from good people.

He told us to have a fun night, and asked Mom if she'd like him to walk her to her car. She seemed charmed, gave me a kiss on the cheek, told me I did a great job, and walked off with him.

Jason turned to me, stuffing his hands into his pockets. "Wow—my dad isn't always that impressed with improv. Crutch-prov wins."

"It almost felt like cheating."

He opened his mouth to say something else, when a girl practically jumped between us, grabbing both of our shoulders and squealing, knocking my right crutch out from under me. Jason's face flashed with concern as he reached out to grab me, but I'd already caught myself with the other crutch.

It was Marissa, the *serious*-theater girl from the beach, and she was oblivious to the fact she'd almost taken me out. "Oh my God, Ellie. You are so funny. I loooooooved your group's set. It was, like, nonstop." She moved her face too close to mine and lowered her voice. "You are so strong. I cannot believe you have cancer. I almost cried for you, but instead you made me laugh, and I simply cannot believe it."

Bam. A verbal joust to the gut. Did she just *tell me* I have cancer? Also? Not sure if I wasn't offended she only *almost* cried for me.

"Who told you *that*?" I asked in such a scathing tone her head jolted back and I had to push back the venom. "I prefer *tumorously challenged*."

Jason let out an airy laugh.

"Oh, um…" Marissa's eyelashes fluttered at warp speed.

"There's no diagnosis yet," Jason said. "Sorry, Ellie, that's probably my fault. The team asked why you were on crutches, and I told them you had a biopsy. It must have spread like the worst game of telephone."

"They're just being cautious. It's probably nothing," I assured Marissa, and myself.

"Well, you are just so brave."

I didn't really see how the misfortune of possibly having a disease made me brave. All that came out was, "Uh…"

Marissa whipped her long, silky braid over her shoulder and grabbed me again. In a teacherly voice she said, "If it is cancer, you should stop eating sugar. Have you already? The only thing I know about cancer is, don't eat sugar. Cancer loves sugar. Cancer eats the sugar right up."

It was so absurd that I couldn't stop my first thought from popping out of my mouth. "Really? That's so weird—I love sugar. Cancer and I must have a lot in common."

Jason stifled a laugh as Marissa's face made a nanofrown. "Oh." Then she hugged me around the crutches. "Well, I'm so sorry you're going through this. I'm praying for you, okay?"

"Thanks, Marissa," I managed as she bounded off.

Jason was covering his mouth with one hand, but the rest of his face was smiling, his eyes crinkling at the corners. "That was solid."

I shrugged. He stared at me intensely. His cheeks reddened, and he crossed his arms, then uncrossed them and put his hands in his front pockets, then shifted them to his back pockets.

"Jason, what's going on over there?" Balancing, I waved my hand around at him.

"Can I show you this cool grove of trees at the side of the building?"

"You want to show me some *trees*?"

"Yeah, I think you'll like them."

I laughed. "Yeah, I definitely want to see these trees. Real bad."

We escaped out the back door of the auditorium, around

to the side of the school, where there was a grassy area lined with the promised trees. Once we were hidden where no one could see us, I teasingly said, "Wow, you were right. I've never seen such a beautiful grove."

He closed the distance between us, moving one of his hands to the small of my back, the other to my neck. He kissed me like every part of him *needed* to kiss me. I let my crutches drop to the ground and, while balancing on one leg and mostly being held up by Jason, I kissed back, my body softening into his hands, into his lips.

He picked me up, fully off the ground, and I let out a little "woo!" in surprise. Then he lowered me onto the grass as if I were one of the early fall leaves being gently guided to the earth by the wind. Because everything in me was wired to ruin moments like this, I said, "Impressive."

"What can I say." Taking the palm of my hand, he traced his fingers along it and up my arm, tingles trailing, adding to the built-up energy from the show. "You were seriously funny tonight. On crutches and everything. You…you're amazing."

My smile filled the whole of me. "Thank you. Not just for saying that. For all of it. These two shows we've done with you have been by far my favorite ever. And I never would've gone up there tonight on crutches if you hadn't…" I trailed off, the happy-weepies choking me up a little. I wasn't used to this. Being with a guy like this. I leaned down and kissed the palm of his hand, a tiny act that, for me, was a thing of boldness. "Just, thank you." And with those three little words came an electric wave of realization. *Oh.* It happened, or was happening. I'd fallen, was falling.

Love. A giddy treasure of a word I was going to keep to myself a while longer.

He beamed and we kissed again until we had to catch our breath. Wrapping me up in his arms, he nestled his face to my neck. Dizzy with it all, I held on to him tight and ran my hand through his soft, perfect hair. The rustling leaves, the warmth of him, the cool night air…I could stay here forever.

We lay back on the grass, side by side, hand in hand, gazing up at the stars. It was a clear night, which was good because I had a lot of wishes to make. Tomorrow might bring good or bad news, but for this one moment it didn't matter. I imagined if we stayed here long enough I could sink into the earth, my sickness melting with my joy, tangling in the tree roots underfoot.

Chapter Twelve

Perched awkwardly on the unforgiving hospital table, I waited for my diagnosis. This room was colder than the rooms I'd waited in before, the air frozen and gray. The confidence I'd felt Friday night with Jason was obliterated by the panic pulling me under.

Dr. Nichols marched into the room, a gaggle of lab coats filing in after, taking positions around the exam table, causing a *whoosh* that sent a chill up my bare legs.

"Good morning, Ellie, Sonia." *That look on her face. I can't take this.* I gripped on to Mom's arm like I was five years old, as she said a quick hello for both of us because I couldn't speak.

Dr. Nichols brought up my MRI scan on a large screen on the wall. "I'm sorry to have to tell you, but the biopsy shows the tumor is malignant. You have a rare cancer called chondrosarcoma—an overgrowth of cartilage in the bone."

Everything in me shattered.

No. No.

Please, please, no.

Mom clutched me to her chest and whimpered as I stared at the scan, a section from my hips to knees. All of the bones were clean and strong-looking…except for one. The left one, bent like a weeping willow, mottled with blackness.

A silent war had been raging in the deepest part of me, my entire femur bone beaten and eaten. I'd had no idea. My poor little bone. It was the saddest, ugliest thing I'd ever seen. And it was inside me. *Cancer* was inside me and, from the image on the scan, it was winning. Ready to take over.

My eyes clouded, and my heart thumped in my gut somehow, all of my anatomy now backwards and misshapen. A voice broke through the fog. "Ellie, we have no other cases with which to compare yours. To help you understand how rare this is, you are one percent of one percent of one percent. Because the tumor takes up almost your entire femur and has curved the bone, it makes the options for surgery more complicated. Chemo and radiation aren't effective with this type of cancer, so wide-sweeping excision is the only way to treat this. There are several procedures we can discuss."

None of this made sense. She had to be wrong.

Mom still had my head pressed to her, and I could hear her breath and her heart rioting inside. In a shaky voice she asked, "Why…why is it malignant? How did she get this?"

"There was nothing you or Ellie could have done. I'm sorry there is not a better answer, but this is an unlucky mutation."

Mom tensed so much she was crushing me. Like if she held me hard enough she could undo this, keep me safe, protect me from whatever was next. "What do we do?" she whispered.

Her face solemn, Dr. Nichols said, "We haven't worked with a case like yours at this hospital before, but options to consider include…" A ringing in my ears made it difficult to focus on the dizzying list of procedures that followed, but I caught some that didn't even sound like real words. *Allograft. Partial allograft. Fibular graft. Arthoplasty. Curettage. Amputation.*

Mom cut her off before she finished. "Excuse me, amputation?" She let go of my upper body and clasped my hand instead. She wasn't technically shouting, but she might as well have been. "Is that a real option? Obviously, we don't want that one."

Dr. Nichols's face twitched. "I understand it sounds scary, but amputation offers the best chance of avoiding a recurrence." She pointed to the scan. "Ellie, because of the tumor's proximity to the knee joint, you need to understand that all the options for limb-salvaging surgery carry the high probability that you will always walk with a limp and never be able to fully bend or straighten your leg again. Most importantly, amputation is the option with the lowest mortality rate."

Saliva flooded my mouth. I swallowed hard to keep from throwing up. *I can't do this. How will I do this?*

"Prosthetics are quite advanced, and it would allow Ellie to maintain her ability to run and jump."

"We'll want a second opinion," Mom said.

"Of course. You'll want to act fast with your decision, but a second opinion is always a good idea. Since her case is so unusual, I recommend we send her scans to one of the big cancer centers—MD Anderson or Memorial Sloan Kettering. We'll give you information to take home and read about prosthetics, as well as a list of the options to review."

They went back and forth with more questions and responses. I tuned out. Then, the appointment was over. Dr. Nichols and her flock of students with their swooshing white coats left us there in the silence, the cold, the never going back.

This time I wished for a wheelchair because my limbs had dissolved into uselessness. Wobbling, shaking, Mom spotting me all the way, we somehow got me dressed and made it back to the car.

When we got in, Mom gripped the steering wheel but didn't turn the key. Through gritted teeth, her voice came out low and determined with a few cracks giving away how hard it was to keep it together. "I'm sorry, Ellie, I'm so sorry. We're going to find you the best doctor…the very best option. Okay?"

She turned to me and pulled me into a hug, which wasn't so much of a hug as us collapsing in on each other, sobbing, desperate, one in our desolation.

Chapter Thirteen

Mom and I spent the rest of the day in her bed. "Are you hanging in there, sweetie? We'll get a second opinion. We'll get through this, okay?"

All afternoon I'd stared out the window, or at the walls with my eyes out of focus, noticing how the pumping of my heart rocked my body back and forth ever so slightly. I'd never been still for long enough to notice.

The pillowcase rustled—sounds were extra loud today— and I turned to look at Mom. Her eyes were red and puffy. I found her hand and held it as cold stones churned in my gut. It killed me that she had to deal with this, too. That my leg had betrayed both of us. That my sickness was causing her so much pain.

I was spacey and out of it, and it was almost like I was in her mind instead of my own, like maybe we were so close we shared this energy field and I could hear and feel her thoughts. You bring a daughter into this world and give her everything you have, all your love. You pray every day for her to be safe and protected. You hold the fiercest hopes that she will have the best life possible. She's been so good, has done so well, worked so hard, seems so healthy and—*wham*. Cancer. Your baby.

Mom squeezed my hand. "I'm giving us today to just be, and then tomorrow I'm doing all the research, calling all the doctors, and making all the plans."

Squeezing her hand back, I stared back out the window.

I hadn't told Jason exactly when I was getting my results, but Hana, Quinn, and Craig knew. I hoped they would give me a day without asking.

Mom took a deep breath and said, "You should call your father and let him know as soon as possible."

I shook my head. Had our sheets always made this much noise? Quietly I said, "He's still in Hawaii until tomorrow." And then, adding the part I still couldn't get over, "He kinda checked out from being my dad when he moved away my last year of high school. So, let him finish his vacation. I'll still have cancer tomorrow." The word practically caught in my throat, and I swallowed down a faint taste of bile.

Mom used her most gentle voice, which I'm sure was hard for her, because she was mad at Dad, too. "Ellie, your dad loves you, and he definitely cares. As for him going on vacation instead of being here for you, I don't get it, of course, but he didn't think it was going to be something so big. None of us did. As for him moving to Wisconsin, I know my words will never make it better, but I think he sees you growing up and no longer needing him. You're busy with all your activities, you're off to college next year, and his choice to follow Barb was his way of looking out for himself."

I had nothing else to say about him, or to him, right now.

Mom's face softened. "Do you want me to tell him?"

"Yes, please."

Mom scooched in closer, nuzzling me into a hug. She smelled like apples and ginger and tissues. She planted her lips on top of my head in a long kiss, and we fell asleep like that, her soft breaths in my hair.

The sound of the apartment buzzer woke me. Mom moved first. "I'll see who it is."

Thank God, because there was zero possibility of me getting out of this bed. My friends were at the door, I was sure of it. My pulse quickened—I wasn't ready, I didn't have words, I couldn't break more hearts right now.

Beep.

Click of the dead bolt.

Silence, waiting for the person, or persons, to get from the front entrance down the hall to our door.

I found a tissue and wiped my eyes and nose, tried to sit up in bed. It was something at least. It was effort.

Doorknob turns.

"Come on in." Mom's voice.

Whispers. Shuffling. Definitely more than one set of feet.

Our apartment is so small that it was only seconds before they were in Mom's bedroom, surrounding me. I got this morbid image of me in a casket, them looming over me with the same expressions that were on their faces now.

I stared at them all, wishing I could pretend to be a corpse with the luxury of not having to speak.

Craig stood with his hands in his back pockets. "So, we're assuming it's bad. Cancer, then?"

I nodded.

Quinn made a choky gasp, kneeled by my bedside and grabbed my right hand, cupping it between both of hers. "We're going to be by your side and do whatever we can," Quinn said.

"Thanks, but there's nothing you can do," I mumbled.

Hana sat on the edge of the bed and put her hand on my leg. "I'm so sorry, Ellie."

Craig blew out a puff of air. "I'm sorry, too, sis. What's the kick-cancer's-ass plan?"

"Tell us everything," Quinn said.

"There's no plan, yet." I somehow managed to ramble off all the horrible words and outcomes Dr. Nichols gave us this morning. "I have to weigh the choices between my life and my leg, so…I'm not real eager to talk about it."

Quinn's porcelain white skin went a shade paler, her softly arched eyebrows knitted, and her little heart lips nearly disappeared into her mouth.

Hana's voice turned to gravel as she said, "Oh, Ellie," and her beautiful brown eyes dimmed with heartbreak.

"That is the roughs." Craig kicked off his shoes and came around the other side of the bed and scooted in until he was next to me, hugging me. Hana and Quinn climbed in, too, until we were in not so much of a sandwich hug, but a pile-of-mashed-potatoes-and-gravy hug.

Every part of me was embraced, making my treacherous body momentarily safe. And in that glimmer of a moment, even with cancer, even with the future so bleak, I had something powerful, something to be grateful for, something not everyone gets in a lifetime, hugging me close.

After barely sleeping all night, the next morning I welcomed the distraction of school. At least I was out of our apartment, but I mostly zoned-out in my classes and tried to avoid everyone's questions about my leg. My last period was my free one, and I crutched backstage for some peace. It was dark, with only enough light from the auditorium seeping in to catch the outline of the furniture and Harold's bowl on a table next to the couch. Quinn had taken him last Friday after the second Mash-Up and promised to look after him, but I'd hated abandoning him. It was weird to think how my tumor was five times as long as Harold's entire body.

I sat on the couch. "Hey, Harold, I don't want to get your fins in a tizzy, but I have cancer." This new word in my life was so much worse than tumor, but it was easier to tell a fish, because fish can't cry. "For real, the actual capital C-word. So, you know what that means? I'm going to be, like, a *gigantic bummer* to hang out with. Fair warning, lil' guy." I inched closer. "You hungry?"

Turning on the small lamp by his bowl, I gasped. "No! Oh, Harold, *no*."

He was floating, lifeless.

"My poor, sweet fish friend." I put my hand on the bowl and sobbed. Goldfish don't live long, but he'd been our mascot since before I joined Spontaneous Combustion. He was my good-luck fish, my confidante. And I'd become the grim reaper, darkness following me and causing pain to everyone around me. "I'm so sorry I dragged you around. It was too stressful for your little body."

The tears dripped into his bowl as I said a prayer. "Dear Harold, thank you for being such a cheerful, bright spot in our lives. You were a good listener, a faithful companion, and the best mascot an improv group could ask for. You helped us have more funny scenes than sucky ones." I sniffled and wiped my nose on my sleeve. "I'm…I'm not sure what awaits a goldfish after…after death…if anything. But may there be something for you, and may it be a magical temperate lake full of other fishy friends. Know your life brought joy to others." My voice faltered, but I squeaked out the last words. "Rest in peace, lil' guy."

Turning off the lamp, the silence of the blackness, the aloneness, hit me. *I have cancer and I killed Harold.* Curling up into a ball on the old couch, I stared at the wood floor with its chipped paint, scuffmarks, and a random shellac of gum, wishing I could seep between the floorboards and disappear.

I have absolutely no control over anything.

That's what I loved about the stage—it was the one place where I had the power to create anything. Real life was the hard part. Onstage I could be someone else, live in a pretend world for a while. I could make goldfish rise from the dead. I could fall in love…and it wouldn't hurt anyone.

Holding my hand to my lips, I thought of Jason in the grove of trees outside of Porter. If only I could return to live in that moment forever. How was I going to tell him? What guy would want to be with a cancer-ridden girl he just met? Especially a guy who just lost his mom to the stupid disease a year ago?

I closed my eyes and clutched a couch pillow to me, wanting to rip it apart.

I'm sorry, Harold.

I woke up on the couch backstage to Craig shaking my arm and Hana saying, "Wake up before the couch-bugs bite."

"We're driving to Craig's house for Las Palomas del Disco rehearsal," Quinn said, doing a poorly exaggerated Spanish accent.

I sat up, groggy and not wanting to deal with their… cheery capableness. "I'm not doing that. Harold's dead. And it's my fault."

"What? No," Quinn said and rushed to his bowl, turning on the lamp to see his tiny orange body floating. "I promise I kept his water clean and fed him. Just this morning he was fine—maybe moving around slower than usual, but alive."

"He looks peaceful," Hana said. "It was his time. That

goldfish lived longer than any goldfish should have. I was starting to wonder if he was supernatural."

"Hana's right. It's not your fault." Quinn hugged me.

Craig sat next to me and patted my good leg. "Harold was a mascot of the performing arts, Ellie. I think he'd want you to go to rehearsal so you can continue to bring joy to the masses through improv and disco."

"Don't make fun." I shoved him. "Plus, I can't dance, ya heard?" I kicked my leg up.

"We have an idea to solve that, and I'm ordering a ton of pizza on Barb's card," Craig said. "The alternative is hanging out with your sad mom at home and researching your sad options."

"Well, when you put it like that." I begrudgingly followed them out to their cars, not sure which was worse: that I had cancer…or that I'd eventually see Jason and somehow have to tell him that I had cancer. I mean, obviously one of them was fundamentally worse. But I seriously doubted my capacity for the other.

No way he's gonna wanna stick around for the horror show that is my new life.

Chapter Fourteen

As we waited for Owen and Jason to show up at Craig's, we stuck our glitter-paper stars on the pant legs of our jumpsuits. I held up one of the shiny gold costumes. "These look amazing, Quinn. I can't believe you made these so fast."

"Thanks. Dad and Gary helped me with the sewing. We brought them over to the theater they're working at and got to use the costume shop there. It was actually fun. I mean, who knew I'd end up liking designing and sewing costumes with my dads?"

I fidgeted with the necklace Hana and Quinn had given me, thinking about all the plans I probably wouldn't be able to be a part of. I realized I missed my turn in the conversation when Quinn spoke again.

"So, how are you going to tell Jason?"

"Yeah," Craig said from his spot at the coffee table with his laptop. "Didn't his mom die of cancer last year?"

I gave him my ice-glare. "Yes, I'm aware of that, which is why I'm not going to tell him."

"What?" Quinn shrieked.

Hana raised her eyebrows.

"Dude, you have to tell him," Craig said. "Doesn't he know you got your diagnosis yesterday?"

"I left it vague when I was getting it, so I bought myself time." I accidentally bent one of the star points I was working on and ruined it forever. *Like everything.* It made me so mad I crumpled the whole thing and threw it against the wall.

No one mentioned my paper-star violence.

"Dude, you have to tell him, or that will for sure blow up on you." Craig pointed at me and then blew it up like Luke had done at the show. I didn't appreciate the pointing/exploding hand thing.

"I don't want to."

Craig, Hana, and Quinn said in near-unison, "You have to."

"No, I don't."

Everyone else: "Yes, you do."

"No, I don't."

"Yes, you do."

We repeated that fun little exchange until the doorbell rang.

Owen and Jason came inside, and with one look at him, everything else—the worries, the reality—drifted away. I stood up to greet them.

Jason's gray T-shirt stretched across his shoulders. *Those are really perfect jeans. How could I just have been given a leg/life sentence and still also feel like this?*

His face lit up, and I couldn't help but smile. I bit my lip trying to keep my grin from getting too big. He crossed the room toward me, my heart seeming to kick up a beat with each step.

"Hey," he said.

"Hey," I said.

He brushed back a piece of my hair. "You okay? Any

news on when you'll get your diag—"

I kissed him. *Dual-purpose kiss: hush up the diagnosis convo, and also, kissing.* I didn't care if my friends got a front row seat to the smooch show.

"Settle down you two," Craig said. "This is serious rehearsal time."

"Evil stepbrother!" I shouted as we broke our kiss. Jason smiled, his hand lingering on my jawline and my heart beating faster at the same time it was breaking from the weight of my news. *Get it over with. Tell him. Just get it over with now.*

Una Paloma Blanca played and Owen clapped his hands and said, "Five, six, seven, eight!" in a joking voice. "No really, what moves did we decide on? I can't remember. Did I ever mention I can't dance?"

"Some truths are self-evident," Jason said.

"Shut it," Owen said.

The five of them showed me the moves they came up with at the last rehearsal I'd missed.

It was a disco disaster. But the shimmies, the glitter, the commitment! There's a saying in improv: if you're going to fail, fail big. "Nailed it," I said, forcing a laugh, hopefully hiding the crushing feeling that I was so separate from them at this moment.

"Okay," Hana, said to me. "Two options for you. We can either do a lot of lifts, carrying you over our heads while you flap your arms like that one dancer in the video who pretends to be the dove, or we could put you on a rolling stool that we'd surround with...wait for it...are you excited to know what?"

She waited for my reply. I shrugged.

"A bird's nest. We'll dress you up as the white dove."

"Pretending to play the flute," Quinn said.

"You mentioned you were quite skilled at pretend-playing the flute," Jason added.

"Either way, we'd dress you up as the dove, whether we

lift you around the room or spin you around in your stool nest." Hana said this like my participation had been decided.

They'd all discussed it and thought about it—about me—and I loved it at the same time I hated it. The special cancer girl in a *bird's nest*? This had to be a new low. Plus, would I even be going to the contest? Or would I be having my leg amputated? They were all trying to make me feel included and distracted. But none of this mattered.

Holy crap, I felt weepy-pukey.

"Yeah, maybe. I'll think about it. Thanks," I managed to get out as I realized I'd accidentally bent another paper star. I smoothed it out and pasted it to the jumpsuit anyway.

The pizza finally arrived and we got to take a break from rehearsal. Everybody talked and laughed, and I tried my best to keep up and put on a good show.

When we finished eating, Owen lifted up his shirt, patted his stomach, and said, "Ugh, so full. But my belly really wants that last slice." He squished his midsection together until his belly button looked like a mouth, which he engaged in conversation. "Hey, Belly, are you hungry?" It turned out Belly was, and demanded to be fed directly. Owen, the belly ventriloquist, said in a deep voice, "Feed me, Owen. Feed me." Dutifully, Owen took the pizza slice and shoved it into his "belly-mouth."

It was all so gross and funny that I laughed, for real.

We all did, until Owen finally took the pizza out of his belly button.

"Ow, my stomach hurts from laughing," Quinn said, clutching her sides.

Owen was so unlike the boys Quinn usually crushed on. He was goofy, kind, and I'd never seen a guy make her laugh so hard. I wondered if they'd last. I wondered where any of these new friendships would be next year.

"So, Owen," I said, "is franchising the Pizza Belly Workout in your future, or do you have something else planned after graduation?"

He leaned back, tipping his chair onto two legs. "The usual summer of chasing rich people's balls." He waited a beat for us to groan. We obliged. "Caddying, that is. Then to college to study physics," Owen answered.

"*Physics?*" Quinn's face crinkled up.

"It's official. I'm one hundred percent surrounded by nerds." Craig sighed.

"Again, I ask: physics?" Perched on the edge of her chair, wearing a plunging wrap dress, Quinn looked beautiful. "I figured you would go into comedy, or follow your dad in his business."

"Somehow Owen's dad suckered us into going to summer physics camp years ago—" Jason said.

"Physics *camp*?" Quinn cried.

"I know," Owen said. "I know, but it was awesome, and Jason and I have been secret geeks ever since."

"Yeah," Jason added, "Except the part about it being a secret. I still like physics, and it would be the smarter choice for a college major, but I want to give film a chance." Jason shrugged and looked up at the ceiling. I imagined him thinking of his mom every time he looked up like that.

"Why film?" I wanted to ask more questions, wanted him alone, to myself, to learn everything about him. *But what's the point now?*

"My favorite things are art, music and…" He looked at me in a way that made me hope he was thinking "and you." "And improv. I like the idea of combining all of that in film. Have you heard of The Neutrino Project? They do improvised shows where an audience is in the theater and the group is out on the streets with cameras, and live video feeds to the theater. So cool." He shrugged again. "Something like that, but maybe longer, less ephemeral."

Did he just talk about an improv form I didn't know even existed and then end on the word ephemeral? Swoon.

"And you, Quinn?" Owen asked.

"I'm not ready for college yet. I want to travel everywhere I can, first." She spread her arms out wide.

They all talked about their top school choices, college goals, plans for the end of high school. I was thankful no one asked me. I was the tumorous elephant in the room, and no one dared question my future. Looking around at Jason and my circle of friends, I realized how much I would miss this. Miss them. It was all so fleeting...so ephemeral.

Standing up, I tucked two empty pizza boxes between my arms and crutches and took them into the kitchen to a chorus of protests. After folding them into the recycling bin, I turned around to see Jason standing close. He set the plates he'd brought in on the counter.

"That was a valiant and unnecessary effort." His smile showed off his irresistible one-sided dimple. He did his hand-brushing-back-his-hair thing, like he was *trying* to make me faint off my crutches. "Why'd you leave just then?"

It took me a second to pull my focus from his handsome face and realize I must have left the conversation at an odd time. "Oh, you know, sometimes I like to ruin things I'm enjoying by getting a jump on missing them already." I hoped he would think I meant because it was our last year of high school and everything would change for everyone.

But his face shifted from teasing to serious, and he said, "Ellie, did you get your diagnosis or something? You seem different, sadder."

Craaap. "I just did. Yesterday. I'm still digesting it. I wanted to tell you in person, but not with everyone around.

Well, honestly, I didn't want to tell you at all." I laughed, sniffed, blinked fast. The tears were coming—*no, no, no*.

Una Paloma Blanca started up again in the living room. *Seriously the wrong soundtrack for this moment.*

"Tell me," he whispered so sweetly.

I held myself steady and forced the tears back. "Yes, it's… it's cancer." His face became a riot of micro-expressions, but I persisted. "A rare bone cancer. I totally understand if you—"

The front door opened and Barb hollered, "*What* is going on here?"

Chapter Fifteen

Jason and I bolted into the living room to see Barb looking like an enraged clown with her orange hair, purple power-suit, and reddening face. Dad stood right behind her carrying giant suitcases and wearing his concerned frown.

I stopped too abruptly, my swinging leg creating momentum but my crutches creating drag. Jason caught me before I face-planted.

I could see how the house must look through our parents' eyes. Blaring music. The rest of the pizza mess still covering the dining table. Piles of gold jumpsuits, fifty glitter-paper stars, and bottles of fabric glue strewn across the entire dining room and living room area. The couches, coffee table, and end tables overflowing with our bags, books, and snack remnants.

Barb's nostrils flared. "Craig Jordan Kowalski, I thought I could trust you. There's no excuse for trashing my house and having parties without permission."

He stood up to his full height. "What are you even talking about? This isn't a party. We're working on a project. Also, you didn't ask *my* opinion when you decided to abandon me in this house and barely come back, did you?"

Barb recoiled, then recovered. "No excuses. This is unacceptable. Unacceptable!"

"In case you haven't noticed, there are some intense things that have been going on in our lives, mostly—um, wait, let me think—oh yeah: *Ellie having cancer.* And what have you two been doing for her? *Nothing.* Lounging by the ocean while she fears for her life." Craig's voice cracked. "We're all just here, hanging out, trying to get through this together."

My eyes and nose prickled.

"Don't speak to your mother that way, son," Dad said.

"You don't tell me what to do, and *don't* call me son. How can you stand yourself? You've barely even checked in on her. You haven't shown up."

Dad's face tensed. Instinctively, I almost defended him, but then I realized I had nothing to say. It was true. He didn't come home early, because it was inconvenient. Barb and Dad hadn't even come back every weekend from Wisconsin like they'd promised.

"Can we talk about this outside, Mother?" Craig asked, pulling out a low but scathing tone on the word "mother." Barb marched past him, heading through the kitchen toward the backyard.

I tried to get a gauge on my dad. He hated conflict. Through a tense jaw he said, "You two are out of line to be inviting this many guests over without asking, and to speak to Barb that way—"

No way. I was having none of that. My crutches stabbed the floor with each step back to the kitchen. Through the large window to the backyard, I saw Barb and Craig, and I gathered from their wild gesturing that their conversation wasn't going well, either.

We cleaned up in speedy silence—me ignoring Dad when he tried to speak to me again—gathered all our stuff, and walked out to the driveway.

"We need to talk some more. Call me later?" Jason asked. I nodded. I craved for him to hug me, but he gave me the quickest kiss on the cheek and headed to his car to wait for Owen, who was finishing up a drawn-out good-bye with Quinn.

Hana huffed up to my side, crossing her arms and narrowing her eyelids at the house. "I'd tell that Barb off if it would help."

"I'd torpedo kick her to the moon if it would help. My dad, too." I couldn't believe him. "Maybe I should ask if a bionic leg is an option? That would be handy right now."

"Now you're talking," Hana said as we walked over to Quinn's car. When she finished her good-bye with Owen, she got in the car and pulled out of the driveway fast, in a fleeing-the-scene-of-a-crime way.

"I feel for Craig," I said. "How did he turn out so well with her for a mom?"

"Do you think he'll be okay?" Hana asked. "He always seemed tough, but the more I get to know him, he's pretty sensitive, huh?"

"He really is." I nodded.

Quinn poked Hana on the thigh. "I think he just needs some *lurrrvin'* from you. It'll make everything better."

Hana shoved her and, flustered, turned again to where I sat in the back. "I don't want to talk about this. Too weird."

"You know I'm happy for you two," I said. "So, talk away. Especially because I'm looking forward to the height-challenges of your relationship."

Quinn laughed.

"Shut up, you guys." Hana glared at me and slapped Quinn on the leg.

Quinn dropped Hana and me off at our adjacent apartment complexes, and we said our good-byes.

When I got inside, Mom was in her bedroom with the light on. "I'm home," I said in passing, heading straight to my room and flopping down on my bed, though I knew I wouldn't be able to sleep.

I pushed the heels of my hands against my eyes to stop the images of me breaking the news to Jason in the kitchen when Barb started screaming her orangutan face off.

Mom knocked on my door. "Sweetie, your dad's here to see you." I widened my eyes and shook my head at her, but she wasn't going to have it and widened her eyes right back at me, a look that made it clear I had to go see him.

Dad was standing in the living room, and I peered around suspiciously for Barb, but she wasn't there. I wondered if she and Craig were still at it, or if she was waiting, or rather, fuming, in the car. Dad's face was constricted. I glared at him.

"Craig is right," he said.

I narrowed my glare even more. "What do you mean by that?"

"Back at the house, I was getting to it, but I should have said that first. Craig is right. I haven't been there for you, and I'm sorry."

My eyes welled up. Those were the words I hadn't known I needed to hear so badly. I took a deep breath and tried my best to suppress any tears. After Barb's freak-out, the way he and Barb had abandoned Craig, and him not coming to see me sooner, I wasn't going to just let it go. That was some pretty unforgiveable stuff.

Mom gestured to the couch. "I'll give you two some time." Dad and I shuffled over silently and sat down as she retreated to her room.

There was a long pause before Dad said, "I'm also sorry for what happened earlier at the house. Barb is, too."

I nodded.

"You look great, by the way. I'd never suspect you were a cancer patient." He tried to sound upbeat, but the tear that escaped gave him away. My father never cried. Did he actually care? Then why the silence over the past weeks? I was pretty sure cell phones worked in Hawaii.

He rubbed his face and said, "I have a lot of excuses, none of them acceptable. All to do with my own inability to deal with these emotions." A second tear dropped. "Remember that time when you were choking on a string of pizza cheese at your birthday party, and I pulled it out of your throat?

"Or that time you skidded out into the street on your bike, and I reacted in an instant and picked up you and the bike and all before you got hit? This time…" His shoulders drooped. "This…I don't know. I was in shock. And I didn't handle it the right way. I didn't handle it at all. I'm sorry for that. I'm sorry I couldn't protect you from this."

He hugged me tightly, and my chin trembled against his shoulder. I wished he could save me from this, too.

We ended up talking for over an hour. He told me how it had been a stressful time for him and Barb with the move and job transitions. How he missed me. How he had regrets about the timing of their move, but how the slower pace of life in Wisconsin was a welcomed change.

I filled him in on the tumor stuff and told him about some of my favorite moments of our Spontaneous Combustion shows, trying my best not to directly point out he'd missed my performances.

It was getting late when Dad stood up. "I should get back to Craig and Barb. We've got some things to work out, too." He cleared his throat. "I know I haven't handled things well between us, Ellie-bee. I'm going to do better." He looked me in the eyes but stayed quiet. I nodded and waited until I understood he was done with his big speech. We hugged good-bye, and I closed the door behind him, feeling at least a little better about us.

Jason on the other hand... My stomach coiled at the thought of telling him the details. I took out my phone and saw I had a missed call and a text from him.

This was something I had to do in person. I needed to see his face to know how he really felt. I texted back.

Hey, sorry. Just got done talking with my dad for forever. Emotions are hard. Sorry Barb's wrath cut us off. I'm about to fall over from exhaustion. Can we talk tomorrow? Your house sometime after school?

He texted right back,

Anytime. Glad you and your dad got to talk.

Thanks.

I watched the bubble of dots as he typed more, picking at the cuticle of my thumb in anticipation.

Ellie, I'm so sorry it's cancer. I wish I could take your cancer, put it in a beach bag...and throw it into a fiery volcano.

:) I'll research that option, I texted back.

For real, I'm sorry, and I'm here. Talk tomorrow.

How was he so nice? Especially when he'd so recently lost his mom. Maybe that was it—he was trained in all the things you say and don't say when someone drops the C-bomb. He knew what to say to me. What he really thought was probably "Run away."

You're the sweetest, Jason. Goodnight.

Goodnight.

Despite feeling like I'd been up for eighty hours, I slept fitfully with nightmares of volcanic tumors exploding and killing everyone around me, of Jason being carried away in a lava flow, and me, arms outstretched, unable to save him.

Chapter Sixteen

Mom and I sat across from each other at the dining room table. She was in her new permanent position with her laptop, where she'd been for the last few evenings after work, researching and making cancer-parent connections online.

I scanned the spreadsheet I was creating with all the different types of surgeries and their risks, thinking I'd finish a few more rows before going to Jason's, but I couldn't focus on any of the words on the screen with my heart thumping in my gut.

"Mom, can I borrow the car, please?"

She looked up from her screen, her forehead still a sea of lines from over-concentrating on whatever she was reading. "Are you sure your leg is okay to drive?"

I slid her glasses to her across table. "It's my left leg, Mom. I don't need it for the pedals."

"Oh, right. Okay, honey." She got up and kissed and hugged me like she'd never see me again, which I guess was a near possibility.

I went back to my room, brushed my hair, and tried on

seven different shirts in search of the one that best said *I might have cancer but look how cute I am.*

When I got close to Jason's, the sun was setting over the lake, and pinks and oranges lit up the sky. Families biked on the path along the water. The world continued on, even though my life had irrevocably changed. At a stoplight, I stared at my legs and wondered if I'd find a second opinion that would keep me from losing my leg forever. What would a prosthetic feel like on? What would it feel like when I took it off and nothing connected the left side of my body to the earth?

A few minutes later, Jason's dad answered the door. "Ellie, hello. Come on in. Looks like those crutches are making you buff."

"Yes, I'm getting the shoulders I need to fulfill my body-builder destiny."

"Just what you always hoped for," he said drily. "Jason is working in the garden with Olivia. Head on back."

"Thanks, Mr. Cooper." Jason's dad retreated to his office, and I crutched down the long hall past the kitchen. This time I noticed their family pictures along the walls. I paused to look at a professional photo of the four of them taken in the gazebo of their garden. Next to it was a portrait of Jason's mom, this one a natural shot, a black-and-white close-up of her laughing. She was a true beauty, and I saw where Jason got his smile and his singular dimple. At the bottom were the words, "In loving memory of Linda May Cooper."

Every day. Every day he must see this and miss her, wish for one more hug.

I sniffled and moved on to the library. The French doors were open to the backyard.

"Do it now, before either of you gets hurt." It was Olivia speaking from outside. I froze.

"No way. You don't get it." Jason sounded wounded.

"Do you remember what you were like when Mom was going through all that? You're lucky the school didn't make you repeat junior year. Your senior year is just starting and—"

"Stop it. It's not going to be like what Mom went through."

"You don't know that, Jason. Cancer is cancer."

"How cruel would that be? And anyway I—"

"Think about it. What if she has to go through chemo, radiation, surgery? Are you even capable of being that support person right now—again? So soon? It's not fair to you, and it's not fair to Dad and me. You were practically catatonic for months. We just got you back."

Pressure flooded my nose and eyes, and my body shook. I slowly moved out of the library and then crutched down the hall as quietly as I could manage to the front entrance, wishing I could run. My breathing was so fast I could hardly get control of it. I had to leave. *But I told him I was coming. His dad knows I'm here.*

Footsteps down the hall behind me. *Crap, crap, crap.*

Wiping away the pools from eyes, I did my best to steady my breath and my trembling chin. I put my hand on the doorknob like I had just let myself in—*weird, but there are zero un-weird options right now*—and turned around.

"Hey, you're here. Hi," Jason said.

He had a spot of dirt on his forehead. My hand lifted an inch before I resisted brushing the smudge away, resisted kissing him. That couldn't happen ever again. *How cruel would that be?* he'd said. *Right.* I would be the cruel one to let him stay with me out of guilt.

He reached out to what? Touch, kiss, hug me? I don't know. I crutched a step back, not letting him. "Are you okay?" he asked.

Well, that was easy to answer. "No, I'm not, actually. I...I'm sorry to do this, but—"

His face blanched. "No, Ellie don't." He reached again,

grazing my arm as I pulled away.

I had to close my eyes to say the words. "I didn't get a chance to tell you everything. Yes, it's cancer, but it's bad. I mean"—I opened my eyes, keeping my gaze down—"not that all cancer isn't bad, but mine is really rare, and the doctor didn't even know what to do for sure, but her recommendation was"—I took a deep breath—"amputation. So, I can't handle that and do this…" I waved my hand, indicating him and me. "Whatever this is between us."

"I'm sorry, Ellie, so sorry. But please, I—"

"I hope you understand. This is just going to be a lot, and I need, you know…I need to focus."

"I'm here for you. I can help." He looked at me like I was stabbing him.

My insides twisted, but I shook my head, thinking of everything Olivia had said. I was the worst possible person for him right now. My body ached to hug him, but I needed to do this.

"I don't want that from you." I forced the words out. "Please. And I'm not going to do the sketch for the contest." I decided there on the spot. I had no desire to be hoisted over my friends' heads or spun around on a stool in gold lamé. "So, I probably won't see you for a while. I'm sorry. I have to go."

Shaking again, I turned to leave as Jason said, "Ellie, please. Can we talk? Please—"

It was so hard to ignore the pain and pleading in his voice, but I shut the door and crutched as fast I could to the car.

Unbelievable. I can't even run right now.

The second I turned on the ignition, I pressed on the gas. The wheels screeched against the pavement, and I fought to get my seat belt on as I swerved out of the driveway. The longest driveway in the history of driveways.

Back on the road, I opened the windows and turned the music up and up. The shaking got worse until my whole body was sobbing, the tears coming so hard and fast I could barely see. A floodgate opened in my sinuses and snot poured down my mouth and chin.

I searched for tissues, but there weren't any, so I used the bottom of my T-shirt to try and staunch the flow, but it was useless. Like everything.

I was disgusting. And I had cancer. I was a tumorous, slobbering, snot-producing, fish-killing, heart-breaking wreck of a human.

Chapter Seventeen

Hana, Quinn, and I were all in Craig's kitchen on a non-rehearsal night. It had been a week since fleeing Jason. He'd called and texted, and I'd texted back, keeping it short and mostly saying stuff like, "Sorry, I can't. I hope you understand." Awful. But I didn't know how else to keep it together. The sobbing fit on the way home from his house had hollowed me out, and I needed to stay that way. Empty. Numb.

On nights there weren't Las Palomas del Disco rehearsals, Craig and I would come to his place after dinner with Mom at our apartment. There was more room to study, and Quinn and Hana would join us. We did study, but we'd also finish our nights watching a couple of episodes of *Ranma* and overeating Marshmallow Mateys.

Tonight, we were temporarily out of cereal, so we'd made brownies instead.

"Why won't these finish baking already?" Hana's face was practically pressed to the oven door. She was wearing a shirt of her own design that read, "Tiny animals are my friends," with an arrow pointing to a bird that rode on top of a kitten that rode on top of a bunny.

"Probably because they've only been in the oven for five minutes." Craig took a break from messaging with Luke about music to offer his logic. This whole Hana-Craig combo still had my head spinning.

Craig and Hana had gone to downtown Chicago on their date, to the Lords of Misrule concert. Hana declared the date to be "Categorically the best night of my life. The Lords of Misrule is the best band I've ever seen, and Craig the best kisser I've ever known."

(To which I'd responded, "Ew," and, "It's not like you've had a lot of comparison." To which she'd responded, "Eat a bag." To which I'd responded, "Promise to never say that again and I will allow you to keep dating my brother." To which she'd responded, "*Step*," and, "But okay.")

They were now An Item. And while I couldn't quite get over the odd coupling—five-foot Hana nestling in close to six-foot-five Craig—they were also adorable.

"I'm not looking for brilliant answers here. I'm looking for ways to open up the space-time-brownie continuum so I can be in gooey chocolate heaven *now*, thank you," Hana huffed.

Quinn looked up from where she sat at the island counter working on costumes for the sketch. "Seriously, Hana, why are you freaking out over brownies?"

"Nerves, people. Comedy Hub's contest is a little over two weeks away, and everything's a disaster. I only have three quarters of the contestants I need. Do not deny a talent coordinator her chocolate treats." Of course, once she was involved in the sketch, she'd immediately inserted herself into the production side of things, working directly with the Comedy Hub contest producers to be the local high school talent coordinator. When I asked her why she was adding so much to her schedule all at once, she replied, "It's my fate. It's in my name: Hana—*one*. Yoon—*to rule*."

At least she'd use her power for good.

"Won't you please sign up for the standup contest, Ellie?" Hana asked. "It doesn't require any dancing, and you'd be so good."

"Sorry, no way. I'm deciding the fate of my life and limb, and you want me to write a bunch of jokes?"

Not swayed by my dramatics, she gave an even nod. "I do. Sometimes you have to leap and do great things before you are ready."

I shook my head and snorted. "Love ya, but no. Sometimes it's better to never risk than to do a lot of work and risk making a fool of yourself. Is that how that quote goes?"

Hana glared at me. "No. Not even close. And that's the worst, most not-you thing I've ever heard. Take it back."

"Fine, I take it back. But seriously, I might implode if I have to think about anything else right now."

"Grr."

"Hey, Ellie, would you look at this?" Quinn asked, saving me from Hana's wrath. I used the counter as my support and hopped over on my good leg to see the new costume she was working on for Hana. She'd decided on something different than the jumpsuits the rest of them would be wearing.

She angled her laptop toward me.

"Awesome. It's perfect. I can't wait to see it under the lights."

She brightened. "Owen and I came up with the idea together." It came out as a wistful sigh. I was happy for her, yet slightly barfy at the same time. It was like *Midsummer Night's Dream* around here, with me cast as Puck, alone and possibly responsible for all the trouble.

I considered everyone around the island. Craig had his music, Hana had her contest-recruitment ideas sprawled out all over the island, and Quinn her newfound knack for costume design. And what did I have? A list of horrible options for my leg and the latest article I was reading about cancer. Oh, and best of all, my constant companion—fear.

Quinn pressed her lips together. "I wish you'd be part of the sketch. We can do something different that you'd like more."

"I'm good. But thanks."

She narrowed her eyes at me like she wasn't satisfied with that answer, but she didn't push it. "Well, I guess that's all I can do on the costumes for now. So, it's either work on my college app or see if Owen's on his way yet." She grinned with the obvious answer and grabbed her phone. Apparently, Owen was a true romantic. It was weird to see the change in Quinn—she was serious about a guy, one who didn't look like he'd walked out of the crew pages of an ivy-league college catalog.

In just a few weeks, my friends seemed more grown up, more focused, getting ready to start their lives after high school and working on their dreams, while I was stuck in a medical abyss, my free time consumed by research and worry.

Stop it, Ellie. Stop the pity-fest.

I turned to check on Hana and her brownie-sitting.

"How have the last two minutes been?"

"Not good, Ellie. Not good," she said, her gaze at the oven set to laser-beam-kill. With another huff, she walked over to my station at the counter and sat on the stool next to me, her shiny black hair swishing along her shoulders. She peered at the spreadsheet of all the treatment options I'd gotten from Dr. Nichols, along with their pros and cons on my screen. "Okay, I love you, Ellie, but seriously, you're such a nerd." She shoulder-bumped me and said, "What have you found out so far?"

"That none of Dr. Nichols's options appeal to me even a tiny bit." I stuck out my tongue. "But look at this." I maximized an article on my screen to show her. "'Top Ten Miracle Doctors in the United States.' There's this surgeon, Dr. Ray, who cured a woman who had the same type of cancer. Every other doctor told her they would have to amputate her leg."

Hana's eyebrows raised. "That could be you. Why are they so big on amputations? It seems that should have gone out of style in the late eighteen-hundreds."

"I know. Anyway, Dr. Ray did some crazy experimental procedure and was able to save her leg."

"That's awesome. Let's get him to be your doctor."

"Not so easy." I shook my head. "He's at a hospital in New York City."

"We can get you to New York, right?"

Craig chimed in, "Yeah. It'll be a cancer adventure. A *can*venture."

I gave Craig my Displeased Ice Princess glare.

How many words are we going to warp with "cancer" now?

Was this a general thing, or specific to myself and my weird circle of people? Would we have a party on the eve of my surgery and call it a *cancerbration*? A year from my now, will we remember my *cancerversary*?

"Or maybe he could at least refer you to someone that's just as good near here?" she suggested.

"Maybe." I tried not to sound forlorn.

For a minute, we just stared at the article about the miracle doctor. Then Hana turned to me, deeply serious, "Do you think the eggs in the brownies have cooked through, at least?"

"Excuse me?"

"I think they have." Hana hopped off her stool, slipped on the oven mitts and pulled the brownies out of the oven. "How's *that* for problem solving? I have no answers for getting Ellie to her miracle doctor, but I have the power to transform brownie batter into brownie pudding."

We all clapped for Hana as she came to the end of the counter where Craig was sitting, climbed on a stool, and set down the pan. She dug in for a spoonful and blew furiously at her brownie glop. "Now I have to wait for them to cool?" She growled again. "Craig, let's never run out of Marshmallow Mateys again, okay?" She patted him on the knee.

"I promise you, Hana, from now on I will always provide endless bags of Mateys." He gave an endearing smile.

Despite the scalding state of the brownies, the smell of the rich, sweet chocolate lured Quinn and me to join Hana around the brownie soup. We scooped the gooey mess into our mouths with wooden cooking spoons. I had one spoonful and called it good, Marissa's inane words about cancer and sugar niggling at me. But they acted like it was a fight to the brownie finish.

"You two are sugar vultures," Craig said. His knee was pressed up to Hana's thigh.

The only sound for a while came from the pan sliding against the counter as it got pulled back and forth between Hana and Quinn. Finally, Quinn set her spoon down with a groan and went back to her phone. Hana kept at it. I looked at Craig who was texting like crazy.

"What are you and Luke working on?" I asked.

"Music for the Comedy Hub contest."

"What do you mean? I thought you finished the *Una Paloma Blanca* track?"

"I did."

"Okay, so is this something else? Is it a humorous song or something?"

"Hell no." He didn't look up from his phone.

"Sooo…?"

He finally set the phone in his lap, giving me his attention. "I figured with the freaky girl-chip you three have you'd know about it already. The Comedy Hub people asked Scared Scriptless if there were any local high school musicians who could play while the contest judges made their decisions about the winners at the end of the show, and Jason asked me."

"Wow, that's so cool." And then, out of nowhere, big gloppy tears sprouted out of my eyes. I got up, balancing on one leg, balling my fists into my eyeballs. "Sorry, sorry." I grabbed my crutches and went through the kitchen door into the backyard.

This didn't make sense. I was happy for Craig. Happy for all of them.

Am I really so selfish that my friends tell me good news and I cry?

It was a cloudy night. I sat down in the grass, feeling a quick shock of pain around my knee. I adjusted my leg and ripped up the grass. Ripping, ripping, ripping, deeper until I was pulling out mounds of earth, ripping until there was a big circle of dirt in front of me. They didn't understand, they couldn't understand. Or maybe it was me. Maybe I didn't understand. Anything.

"Barb is going to be pissed about the hole in her yard." It was Craig, and I ignored him. He plowed on. "Dude. I'm sorry I didn't tell you. I didn't think it was a big deal. Jason just asked, which is why Luke and I are working on it so fast. You three tell each other everything, I honestly thought you knew and didn't care."

I squished some dirt. "Craig, I think it's awesome, really. I'm happy for you, and I'm seriously not mad you didn't mention it." He plopped in the grass next to me. "I don't know why I reacted like that. Maybe it's because—"

"You have cancer. You pushed away the boy you like a lot. Your friends are doing normal things, and you're stuck on crutches with no answers."

"Yes. *That.* You're annoyingly perceptive."

He shrugged. "That's how I'd feel. Except the part about the boy, or the girl, if it were me."

I arched an eyebrow at him. "Are you about to give me advice about guys?"

"Who better?"

"Anyone besides my stepbrother who is dating one of my best friends?" I shivered involuntarily.

"I'm just saying it doesn't sound like Jason wanted to be pushed away. You act like it's some noble, wise thing you've done, but I call total bull."

"It's not. It's real."

"No one knows the future. If I were you, I'd say, 'Jason, let's carpe diem the crap out of everything before my surgery—no strings, yo?'"

I belly laughed, looking up at the sky, my mouth wide. "So, romantic. Is that what you said to Hana when you ran after her?"

"Hana? No. I didn't think I had a chance with her since she's so out of my league, but I'd follow her anywhere next year if she'd let me. Doesn't hurt she happens to want to go to school in New York City."

My eyes and nostrils prickled. *That's the sweetest thing ever.* "Are you *in love*?"

"I'm just saying I'm in if she'll have me, for as long as she'll have me."

I hiccupped with a cry-laugh that I shook off as fast as it came. "I *cannot believe* you spend your time on abstract music crap when it turns out you could be topping the charts with the sappiest love songs ever recorded. *You're* a hopeless romantic." I poked my finger into his arm. "Holy crap. My whole world is crumbling."

"Eat a bag." Craig shoved my shoulder and made the back-of-the-throat clicking sound he did when he was uncomfortable or embarrassed.

I blew some breath-giggles through my nose and shoved him back. "Eat a bag, yourself."

"Let's keep this heart-to-heart stuff between us for now, okay?" He stood up and stretched his legs. "I'm going back in to see if I can save her from a brownie coma."

"I'll be in in a minute." I rubbed my leg, putting both palms on my knee and feeling the warmth of my hands around the tumor spot. I tried to stuff all the grass back on the dirt mound. It didn't look great, but at least the torn-up ground wasn't so exposed.

I eased myself onto my back, moving like I belonged in a nursing home instead of high school. The night sky was splotched with drifts of gray. There was only one visible star, probably a planet or a satellite. I chose to believe it was a star. The rhyme Mom always chanted on starry nights came to me. "Star light, star bright, first star I see tonight, I wish I may, I wish I might, have the wish I wish tonight."

I closed my eyes, thinking of Mom, of college, of all my friends finding love. Of Jason. Of my unknown everything. *Please, please…heal me.*

Chapter Eighteen

Everyone else had rehearsal for Las Palomas del Disco, so I was sitting on my bed surrounded by my spreadsheet, articles, and piles of the most depressing papers ever from the hospital. *So you have cancer…* Thrilling titles that made me start to regret my decision to drop out of the contest. But it made it easier to keep Jason at a distance if I didn't have to actually see him. I replayed his sister's words in my mind to remind me why I was doing this.

By eleven p.m., I was still wide-awake when my phone beeped. It was a text from Jason.

Are you awake?

Hi.

Don't be scared, it's me. Knock, knock.

There was a tapping on my window. Despite the warning, I bolted up in fear. A second later, connecting the sound to the text, I got up on my good knee to pull up the blinds.

Jason was at my window looking adorably disheveled. Now my heart was racing in a whole different way. I unlatched the lock, and he popped his head and half his torso through the cheap, unscreened window.

"Hey," he said, that simple word causing an earthquake ripple from chest to belly.

"You scared me. 'Knock, knock?' That's a creepy, psycho-killery thing to text."

"But it was coming from me. How's that psycho-killery?"

"I don't know. Maybe the psycho killer stole your phone," I said, keeping my voice low.

"Good point. Next time I'll call first so you can approve my voice. Oh wait, that wouldn't work because you ignore my calls."

Ouch.

"Can I come in? This window ledge is slicing my rib cage. I just need to say a few things, and then I'll leave you alone."

"Yes. But be quiet, our walls are binder thin, and Mom's room is right there." I pointed to the wall across from my bed and moved out of the way as Jason slithered in from the window.

He tumbled onto my bed, sending my stacks of paper everywhere and completely squashing the fourth-grade birthday present from Mom: a stuffed hippo that wore a leotard saying *I love to dance.* Righting himself on my bed, Jason removed Stanley from under the small of his back.

He eyed my white cotton duvet and all the pillows in shades of blues and greens. "Should I take off my shoes?" His face flushed. "Not that I have to stay. Long—stay long—I don't. It's just…I don't want to get shoe prints…"

I nodded yes. This was so awkward.

As he slipped off his shoes he said, "Don't ask how this went in my head."

He smelled so good.

"Okay, let me get this out." His gaze was steady and serious. "No."

I waited for him to go on. He didn't.

"No?" I asked. "What are you talking about?"

"No. I don't accept you pushing me away. You said it was because you couldn't handle us while you're going through all this." He gestured to my leg and papers and crutches. "But I've been thinking about this—like, a lot. You overheard me and Olivia talking that day you came over, didn't you?"

I avoided his eyes and bit the insides of my cheeks.

He huffed. "I knew it. But you must not have heard all of it. What I said back to her."

"You said it would be cruel to break things off with me when I'd just learned I had cancer."

He closed his eyes, puffed out his cheeks, and then looked at me again. "I said that for her. But I said more after that. Look, you don't get to tell me how to feel or who to care about. If you tell me right now that you hate me and don't like spending time with me, or that you really can't handle being around me, I'll go away and leave you alone. But you have to be honest. Because I'm here. And I want to go through whatever happens with you. Period. And it's because I like you. A lot. I want to spend time with you, I want to be with you."

I hunched and hid my face in my hands, overwhelmed by the cacophony of emotions inside me. He stroked my hair. He'd meant every word. I'd given him an out, and he didn't want it. He was here because he liked me and didn't want to give up on us.

Now it was up to me.

Pulling myself together, I sniffled and straightened back up, meeting his gaze. "I really like you, too, Jason. A lot, a lot. I just don't know what's going to happen. It all feels half-real right now. I'm on crutches, I have a scar on my leg, but that's nothing compared to what's ahead. So what does that mean for us? What if I have to get my leg amputated and—"

"I don't know how to tell you this, but…"

"What? Just tell me." I pulled a pillow into my lap.

Jason ran his fingers along my calf, sending tingles through my body. "You have gorgeous legs. Seriously gorgeous. But they're not even in the top five reasons I like you. I hope—for you—that you get to keep your leg. But if not, I'll crowd-source robotics-funding for a kick-ass, tricked-out, Transformer-level prosthetic. Okay?"

I laughed. "Okay. But we really don't know what's going to happen with me. What life will be like, what *I'll* be like. So, let's just agree to the now, not to the future. Deal?"

Jason cocked his head and opened his mouth as if to speak, but then closed it again. He simply nodded then, finally, said, "Sure. Deal."

He leaned over and kissed me. It was a long, body-altering kiss that turned into fluttery kisses. After a while Jason pulled back a little and said, "This is even better than it went in my head." He smiled. "I have another thing to say."

"What's that?" I hugged the pillow closer.

"I think you should do the standup contest for Comedy Hub."

My head about spun off. I threw the pillow up into the air as I whisper-yelled. "What? Why? Where's this coming from?"

"You know the number one place it's coming from is Talent Coordinator Hana. She really gave me the sales pitch at rehearsal tonight. But also, your 'cancer and sugar' line to Marissa has popped into my head a bunch since it happened. So that's number two. And number three is probably my wanting to live through you vicariously. My mom and I would think of the cheesiest jokes to entertain her through treatment. Maybe we could work on your set together?"

I picked at the edge of my journal, which peeked out from under a pillow. There were some jokes I'd jotted in there. Well, I don't know if I'd call them jokes yet, but premises, nuggets of things I found so absurd about all this that they deserved a punchline.

Looking back up at Jason I asked, "What were your mom's favorite jokes?"

He shook his head and gave a breathy laugh. "The worst kind. Knock-knock."

He paused, looking expectant.

"Oh, we're really doing this? Okay, who's there?"

"Alma."

"Alma who?"

"Alma hair keeps falling out."

My mouth gaped with a shock-laugh. "That's terrible."

He grinned. "I know. There's more. Knock, knock."

"Who's there?

"Not my knockers anymore."

"Awful. Did she come up with that?"

"Yep, and she had a big fit of giggles after it. Really cracked herself up with that one." He had a small smile and his gaze went far away.

"That's impressive she could laugh at it."

"Yeah, she was amazing."

I put my hand on his knee and held it there as we sat in silence.

He said, "Quinn said you wouldn't be having chemo?"

I nodded. "No, it's so deep in me, chemo would kill everything else before it even started on the tumor."

It was his turn to nod. He was slipping into memory-land, and I wasn't sure if I should help him dig deeper or pull him out of the depths. As he seemed to get further away, I decided on out. Thinking of the jokey improv game One Eighty-Five, my head reeled with ideas. *Cancer, chemo, tumor...*

"One hundred eighty-five tumors walk into a bar. The bartender says, 'What can I get you?' The one hundred eighty-five tumors reply 'one hundred eighty-seven shots.' The bartender says, 'But there're one hundred eighty-five of you.' The one hundred eighty-five tumors reply, 'We're drinking for *tu-mor.*'"

A slow smile morphed across his face. "Was that a tumor math pun? Owen would love that."

"Yeah, but these are all tragically cheesy jokes and I wouldn't do any of them for the show."

Jason brightened. "So, you'll do it?"

Yes, no, yes, no, yes, no. "Yes. I mean, what I have I got to lose? A leg?"

"Yes! No, I mean, no, not the leg. But yes, that you'll do it. Now I'll get my sign-on cut from Hana." He rubbed his palms together greedily.

I gave him the Ice Princess glare I usually reserved for Craig.

Jason laughed and threw a pillow at me. I threw one back. He threw another one, and I caught it. He pushed his hands back on it, and we shoved the pillow back and forth between us, laughing, until I leveraged up on my good leg and pushed the pillow with my body weight and toppled him over. I buried my face in the pillow between us to stifle my giggles.

"Ellie, are you up, sweetie?" Mom called from the hallway.

I reached across the bed and switched off my lamp. We froze. There was a soft knock on my door. "Ellie?" Mom whispered, waited. "Get some sleep, my love."

The lights in the dining room were on. Now that we'd woken her, she was going to be up researching for a while. *Crap.*

Jason tickled my ear with his whispery words. "Let's just lay here until she goes to bed, and then I'll sneak back out, 'kay?"

Smothering a giggle from the tickles, I nodded a yes against his shoulder. We shifted so I was laying on my right side, and he spooned around me, hugging me tight.

His hand moved down my left thigh until he got just above my knee. "Is it here?" he asked, meaning the tumor.

"Yeah," I answered quietly. He didn't say anything as he nestled against my neck. He held me there, wrapped in his arms, the warmth of his hand emanating into the spot on my thigh.

And that's where we slept all night.

Chapter Nineteen

I was finally, *finally* off crutches...and onto a cane. There had to be a joke in there, but after staggering around like a geriatric wizard, I noted zero comedy in my situation. There were only twelve days until the Comedy Hub contest. At least Dr. Nichols said I'd only need the cane for a couple days as I transitioned to walking and got the strength back in my leg.

The night Jason slept over replayed in my mind every day since it happened. The morning after the surprise sleepover he snuck back out the window early, and I'd immediately called Quinn and then Hana.

Quinn had said, "You *slept* with him?"

"*Next to* him, over the covers, with our clothes on."

"This is serious."

Hana had said, "He said he likes you and wants to go through whatever happens with you and then held you all night without making another move? Clearly he's in love with you."

"I wouldn't go that far, but—"

"He held you all night!" Hana shouted through the phone.

Since that night, my feelings for him were stronger than ever. Of course they were. We talked and texted every day between the frenetic pace of school, preparing for the contest, and all the medical rigmarole. So much had shifted in a few days. And things were about to start moving even faster.

Mom had lined up an appointment with the surgeon I'd read about at the top cancer center in New York City. She'd already bought our tickets, scheduled to leave the day after the contest.

I texted Jason the news about my appointment, and he called me on his way home from Las Palomas del Disco rehearsal. "That's the one from the miracle surgeon article you read, right?"

"You're so good. Yeah, and you won't believe the surgery he's recommending. It's called…" I pulled up the email so I could get the words right. "Curettage and cryosurgery with resection and reimplantation. I didn't even know those words existed before today, let alone were something you could do all together, and possibly *to me*."

"Doesn't sound complicated at all. Any ideas for jokes with that one yet, or is it too soon?"

"Too soon. There's just so much to it, it's hard to find an angle. It would involve sawing out my femur, scraping and freezing it, filling it with a protein-putty from my hip, adding a metal plate, and putting the whole thing back into my body. It sounds like something from a science fiction novel, not my actual life."

"Um…yeah, that's crazy. When is one of these doctors going to suggest your bionic leg idea? But I might have a direction for your cadaver bone option."

"What's that?" I wished we were together so I could see his face. I loved how animated he got when he was inspired.

"Maybe you could think about whose bone you might get. Would it affect you in some way? There's gotta be something in there, right?"

"I like that."

"Could a donor bone give you new abilities?"

"Yeah, maybe I'd get a criminal's bone and receive the gift of an evil fury? Or preferably, an Olympic athlete's bone, and I'd get, uh…the ability of super speed? But…just in the one leg, so maybe I'd run super-fast in a circle?"

"Ha. Whose bone would you want?"

Thinking about it for a second, I said, "The bone of a ninja." I sat up on my bed on my good knee, with my other leg extended, and did a little karate chop with my free hand for just myself. "Wouldn't that be cool? My bone would be sullen and mysterious…and then—*ka-pow!*—kick the crap out of things."

"Nice. You've got something there—ninja donor bone."

We went on talking and brainstorming like we did every night, until Jason was home and in bed and my voice was scratchy from laughing and needing sleep.

A million thoughts poked the back of my eyeballs.

I was at Las Palomas del Disco rehearsal to watch their run-through and give feedback before the big night, which was only five days away, but it was difficult to stay focused. I'd talked with two chondrosarcoma survivors today who called me as part of a program to connect cancer patients with survivors. Instead of reassuring me, they'd served me up thirty-one flavors of fear.

During a break, the others went out back for fresh air, and Jason sat next to me on the couch. "You doing okay? Did you talk to those people who had the same type of cancer in their femur?"

I nodded, the tears bubbling up, threatening to spill.

"It wasn't helpful. I spoke with this lady Beatrice, who's in her seventies. I asked her what it was like for her after the surgery—you know, wondering if I'd be able to bike and do improv again."

"What'd she say?"

I imitated Beatrice's voice, speaking shaky and slow. "'Good, good. Though, some days I have to crawl up the stairs, and it's hard to stand on grass and gravel.'"

His eyebrows shot up.

"I know. This is my future? Hard to stand on *grass and gravel*?"

Jason covered his mouth, his eyes wide. "Man, that's unnerving. But she's in her seventies. When did she have her surgery?"

"Six years ago."

"See? I bet she was already having trouble walking. They shouldn't have matched you up with someone so old. That's not going to be you, okay?"

"I also spoke to a woman in her twenties, and that was almost worse because she's not that different in age and it still didn't sound good."

"How so?" He held my hand and waited intently. It was different talking to Jason about this than my other friends, because he got it on so many levels. At first I'd felt bad because it was asking too much of him, but he said it made him feel good to have some use for everything he'd learned and been through.

"She was that patient of Dr. Ray's featured in the article. I was so excited to talk to her because that story is the only thing that's been keeping me hopeful, you know? And..." And then the tears fell. I covered my face, and Jason pulled me into him so my head was against his chest.

"I'm so sorry Ellie. What happened to her?"

I collected myself just enough to mumble into his shirt,

"She's alive, obviously, and cancer-free, but she has to have another surgery because the donor bone she had is being rejected by her body."

Sniffling, I sat up and reached for a tissue, hoping I didn't have snot all over my face, because that's always attractive. Really added to the whole sultry, crying-over-cancer package that I had to offer. "I just feel like, even if I live through this, even if I get to keep my leg, it could take years to recover, and it still might not be over. This might be my life. Forever."

He handed me another tissue.

Great, I probably do have snot on my face.

I wiped every possible spot. *I should invent a snot-bag, like a poop-catcher for horses, but for cancer patients. You just never know when your nose is going to poop out some snot.* "And, I don't know, I just can't help thinking about how this thing got in me, and *why*."

His expression changed, and he stared out the window for a moment before turning back to me. "I remember overhearing my mom ask my dad that question one night."

"How did he answer her?"

"He told her that it wasn't her fault. For good or bad, it's just science. It's a mutation, you know?"

"Dr. Nichols said something like that, too. How did your mom respond?"

Jason gave a wistful smile. "She said, 'Well, I feel so much better. Thanks, dear.' Then there was some laughing that turned into crying, and that's when I went back to my room."

I waited a beat, letting that memory sit between us.

"Why do people like to call us mutants so much?" I asked.

"*You're* not a mutant. But it's true—we're constantly being zapped from particles shooting from the sun, from space, and it's just luck when a particle doesn't hit a cell and cause a mutation. Or unlucky when it does."

"So, you're saying I can blame this all on *space*?"

He nodded. "Yes, exactly. It's space's fault, not yours."

"I am so pissed at space right now." I looked up and shook my fist in space's direction. "I'm totally going to sue space."

He laughed. "Let's write that down."

Mom had made me start seeing the school counselor. Which was fine because she was also our yoga teacher, Mrs. Lahiri. I usually left each time feeling that, for just a minute, I got to escape the cloud of anxiety that followed me so persistently. But today I was really freaking out, and I didn't think she'd be able to help.

"I'm just a wreck. What's wrong with me?" It was the afternoon before the contest, and I was pacing in Mrs. Lahiri's office. If nothing else, I was grateful to be *able* to pace again.

"There are only two days till I leave for my appointment in New York City. One day till the Comedy Hub contest—a show in front of hundreds of people. And T-minus zero seconds until my head implodes."

Mrs. Lahiri audibly sighed at my outburst, but her eyes seemed kindly amused. I went on.

"I can't sleep. The positive side is that it's given me lots of time to work on the material for the show tomorrow night. But the bad part is my stomach is in knots. My heart is constantly beating so fast I think it will bust out of my chest. My leg keeps bouncing and twitching like it's possessed. There's this nonstop stream emanating directly from my brain to my leg… like a sci-fi laser beam…waa-waa-waa…and I can't shut it off. I can't intercept it. Did I do something to bring this on? I still can't believe a cancerous tumor is in there."

"Please. Come lay down on the couch." She patted the cushions. I did what she said. She turned on her funky lamp and turned off the overhead lights, then she came back to sit on her bright red chair with quilted throw pillows.

Mrs. Lahiri's voice soothed me. "Please, tell me your fears and worries as a list. I do not want to hear your stories or judgments of these fears. I want to hear your concerns only as facts. Go."

"That I'll suck at the show tomorrow. That nothing I say will be funny." I took a deep breath and continued. "That I won't be able to make a decision. Or that I'll make the wrong one and won't walk normally ever again, or I'll be left in constant pain, or the cancer will come back.

"I'm worried about Mom. That she's expending all this energy on worrying about me instead of finding what makes her happy.

"I'm afraid I'll lose my friends, my future. Because they're all moving on in life and I'm stuck behind. That I'll never know what I'm supposed to do with my life, and I'll be miserable because of it.

"I'm afraid of what will happen to Jason and me after surgery.

"I'm afraid of surgery. Of being unconscious while someone is opening me up. Of being out of control."

And then it happened. The knot in my stomach loosened the slightest bit.

"Very good." Mrs. Lahiri moved her chair closer to the couch. She handed me a pillow to prop up my head, then placed her hands a few inches away from my temples, just hovering on either side of my head. "Now, close your eyes." I did. The closeness of her hands calmed me. My heart slowed a little and didn't seem like it was going to rocket out of my rib cage. "Do you believe you have a spirit or soul?"

"Yes," I answered without thinking. Did I? I hadn't thought about it much. But the answer came tumbling out, so maybe I did.

"You did not do anything wrong. Cancer is not a

punishment. But I believe that our souls have come here to learn and grow. Some people continue to push aside their experiences and not learn from them, and those people find themselves repeating the same struggle over and over again. But think of those who have come out of a difficult situation the better for it? Perhaps they would not wish to relive it, given the choice, but they are also thankful for the new gifts they received from it."

I thought how life was a teeter-totter, the ups and downs searching for balance, how the moment I found out I had cancer, I was also given this new connection to Jason and Craig.

"These are people who have accepted their challenges. I believe you are one of these people, Ellie."

I wondered if Mrs. Lahiri had put me in some kind of hypnotic state, as a floaty, slightly dizzy feeling washed over me. I was barely in the room anymore.

"Now, go back to the peaceful place you envisioned a few weeks back."

I rekindled the image of the pond surrounded by birds and sunshine and blue sky and the smell of pine trees.

"I want you to visualize what your spirit looks like."

A vision popped into my head. There was a tall, bright figure in white standing—hovering—in the middle of the pond. She was practically glowing. I couldn't see her face. She was holding on to a little girl about six years old with a ponytail, who was wearing a red windbreaker and a serene, joyful smile. I was confused—why did I see two figures? I quietly shared my vision with Mrs. Lahiri.

"Good. Now, in your mind I want you to ask these two souls to help you make a decision."

The prayer came to my mind easily, desperately almost.

Please help, please help me. Please help me make the right choice. The one that heals me perfectly, with no limp or loss or cancer. Please help me to know when I have made the choice, and help me to trust myself.

My whole body went light and tingly like an outside force was surging through me.

"Now. When you are going into surgery, you can ask your spirit to watch over you. Your spirit will not be affected by the anesthesia. It can protect you while your body is under."

That idea comforted me…a lot. It was like I could have some control while totally having to give up control.

"Ellie, I will say a few things now, and you can think of them when anxious thoughts come up." I nodded. "You are safe. You are protected. Life is unfolding perfectly, you can relax and let go."

I repeated what she'd said.

And this weird sense of peace coursed through me.

Let go. And I did. At least, for today.

Chapter Twenty

Driving to Porter Township for the contest, I sat in the backseat of Quinn's SUV with Jason on my right. That entire side of my body was happy because all the bumps and turns made our shoulders, knees, and hips touch. I was barely able to keep up with the conversations because I was focused on the sensations connecting us.

Owen sat up front next to Quinn, while Hana was in the back with us. Jason smelled so crazy good my brain function was failing. I opened the window to breath in the crisp fall air. The changing leaves of the trees created a kaleidoscope effect as we zipped by.

My hand rested on my right leg, lined up with Jason's hand, our pinky-electrons leaping back and forth, sharing space for fractions of seconds at a time. My heartbeat was so loud and fast it was all Edgar-Allen-Poe-obvious in my head.

Everything was intense tonight.

Next week would be an entirely different world for me. If Mom and I liked the surgeon, we might stay in New York City, and then who knew how long it would be before I'd see Jason again? Either way, here or there, surgery was imminent. And what would my body be like after that happened?

When we rolled to a stop, I turned to Jason, and our eyes held like we'd shared something, even though it had been only in my head. Softly, he said, "We're here." Those two little words were like a caress, and in response my chest puffed up and my left hand stroked the side of my neck, as if I needed proof I was still in my physical body.

"We're going to drop you here so you don't have to walk too far," Owen said as he got out and came around to open my door.

"Thanks. So chivalrous," I said as he gave me his goofy grin and took my hand to help me down.

Jason slid out after me and called to Hana. "You coming?"

She was busy texting. "Yeah, but I'm going ahead of you guys. 'Cause, ya know, if I go at the invalid's pace, Craig and Luke's dinners will get cold." We'd dropped off all our stuff for the show earlier in the evening and then ran out to get a quick bite, but our music boys stayed to run sound cues.

"Hey. This invalid has a name, thank you."

She batted her eyelashes at me, grabbed the bag of takeout, jumped out of the SUV, and headed inside.

"We'll meet you guys in there," Jason said as Owen and Quinn drove off to park.

Students and parents walked past us, filing into the school while we stood on the sidewalk, staring at each other. Now I was sure the energy built up between us was real and not just me.

Jason's eyebrow spiked. "Maybe we skip the contest?"

He'd leaned down to kiss me when Mom's voice echoed out, "Ellie? Jason? What are you two doing out here? Shouldn't you be warming up backstage?"

He wants to kiss me, Mom. Go away!

Oblivious, Mom carried on. "I'm excited. You all have

worked so hard, I can't wait to see what you've been up to."
Right now, kissing is all I'd like to get up to.

Instead of the smaller theater space where we'd had the
two Mash-Ups, the Comedy Hub contest was being held
in Porter Township High School's large auditorium, which
had been decorated with ComedyHub.com banners and
balloons everywhere. It was a sold-out show with fifteen
hundred people—students, parents, teachers from Porter and
Northglenn, and people from the community all around the
Chicagoland area. The theater buzzed with excitement. We
even had a celebrity in our midst with Comedy Hub's lovely
Tricia Wilson hosting the contest. The judges were well-known
local Chicago standups and two actors from Second City.

We sat in the first row in one of the side sections of
the auditorium so we could get between our seats and the
backstage easily. Las Palomas del Disco's sketch was up first
after intermission, and my standup set was one of the last acts
of the night, so we had some time to sit and enjoy the show.

Jason held my hand. My nerves had tempered my
hormones enough that his hand in mine as we watched the
competition was comforting instead of mind-altering.

One contestant, from a high school in the city, seemed
like he'd brought at least a hundred fans. You could tell he'd
done standup before—his punchlines were well-timed and
tight, but they were also pretty gross. The funniest contestant
so far was talented enough to intimidate me, but her material
was so self-deprecating it made me sad even as I was laughing.

How would this audience respond to my cancer jokes?
Would they think I was a freak? Would they stare at me in silent
pity? Squirming in my seat, I chomped the inside of my cheeks
and gripped the bull's-head necklace. *I am strong like bull.*

When Hana, Quinn, Owen, Jason, and Craig headed backstage to get their costumes on during intermission, I wished them all good luck and said I was going to go practice my standup one more time. Only Quinn knew my secret.

I met Gary and Steven, Quinn's dads, in Porter's tech director's office in the scene shop. They handed me a huge garment bag and waited for me while I changed. Unzipping the bag and expecting the "elevated bird costume" they'd suggested, I instead found a legit designer wedding dress. I put on the white sleeveless sheath, the silk soft against my skin, hugging me tight through the hips and thighs. There was a high-cut slit on the right side, and from there, layers of silk and sheer fabric flowed around my legs. Delicately, I took out the second piece and slipped my arms through the lace straps of the feathery wings tipped in crystals. After weeks of feeling like a hobbling troll, I felt glamorous instead of tumorous.

I smiled, trying not to tear up from the kindness. *This is Quinn's family's gift to me.*

When I emerged, Gary gasped and clapped. Steven smiled through his trim beard and nodded approvingly as he said, "You look stunning, Ellie. Now sit. We've got more work to do."

There was no mirror in the scene shop so I couldn't see what they were doing, but Steven twisted up my hair and pinned in a crown of feathers as Gary applied my makeup. "I know you have your standup set soon after this number, so I promise I won't overdo it. But I insist on these gems on your face so you will sparkle in the lights. And you can peel them off real quick when you're done, 'kay?"

"'Kay," I mumbled, not wanting to move my face too much with all the fussing.

"All done. *Magnifique.*" Gary took my hand and helped me stand. "Steven's going to attach the feather bustle and train. And here, hon. I know you haven't needed one for a few days, but in case you need the extra support, this prop does double duty as a cane."

He handed me a cane in the shape of a flute—a giant golden flute. I laughed. "You two are amazing. It's all a work of art. Thank you so, so much."

"The dress we had for another show, and we just took it in a smidge. Most of the other props we had, too. We just made some playful adjustments," Gary said, like it was nothing, which it so wasn't.

Steven finished attaching the train of tulle and the bustle of white feathers, which together flowed about six feet behind me. He pointed to the end of the flute. "This is the best part. In the final moment of the number, press this button."

"What will happen?"

"You'll see," Steven said.

They helped me navigate the yards of fabric through the sawdusty scene shop and onto the stage.

"Your disco ball chariot awaits," Gary said.

It was my turn to gasp. "It's gold. It's huge. It's amazing. Is that a seat on top?"

"You betcha. Only the best for you." Gary hoisted me onto the giant gold disco ball. They clicked me into the harness and arranged my wings and train.

"How do you feel? Are you scared?" Steven asked.

I scanned the catwalks high above the stage. "Normally I would be. But fear feels pretty relative at this moment."

"True, true. Remember, fearlessness is not being without fear, but being afraid and doing the thing anyway. Time to fly, hon." Gary said as the rest of Las Palomas del Disco came to take their places onstage behind the curtain where I was perched on my golden ride.

They were all screams, squeals, wide eyes, and slack jaws. This was fun.

Quinn ran up to touch everything. "You look incredible."

"This is…way unnecessary…and totally *psychedelic*," Owen said, apparently getting into his seventies disco character.

Craig grabbed on to the cables and studied them like he was checking on structural soundness. "I can't believe it. I thought you bailed on us."

"Surprise! I didn't want to leave you all doveless. It was all Quinn's idea and Gary and Steven's magic."

Hana clasped her hands together. "Our beautiful white dove. On a giant flying golden disco-ball-of-dreams."

"Places!" the stage manager shouted.

Everyone ran to their spots onstage. Except Jason. He stood in front of me, his mouth still agape. "Ellie, you look… wow. Just wow. Beautiful. This is…I mean. Can I touch this?" He said pointing to my dress.

"Yes."

He slid his hand along my thigh, landing at my hip. I was glad I was sitting down.

"Puuuh-laces, please," the stage manager called again.

"I don't think I can move," Jason whispered. "I'm not going to be able to dance."

I giggled and pushed him away.

The music started, the cables whirring and pulling me upward. Jason took a deep breath and said, "Ellie, Ellie, Ellie," as he scooted away to his starting pose and I ascended into the fly loft, my stomach flipping, my toes tingling. *Okay, I guess it's possible to feel two fears at once.*

The curtains opened, and the minute the lights shone on the five of them, the audience started laughing and howling. Hana was dressed in a poufy brown man's wig and a gold lamé tuxedo that was stuffed in the middle to hide her curves. She looked like a short Korean Elvis. Everyone else was in their gold jumpsuits.

Hana started singing, and Jason, Quinn, Owen, and Craig,

who took my spot in the chorus even though he only wanted to be in charge of the music, did their shimmying and thrusting in a line behind her. It was a glorious sight to behold.

Hana was hamming it up as only Hana could, and the other four were totally in sync, smiling and hitting every cheesy foot stomp and finger point in time to the music.

About a third of the way into their number, I was flown in. Gripping a cable with my free hand, I braced myself and let out an "Eee!" I hoped no one heard. Swooping over the stage, it was like being on a swing carousel. So fun. The wooziness gave way to giddiness, and I pulled myself together and tried to look dove-like, trusting the harness and letting go of the cable to pretend-play my giant flute. The audience oohed and clapped as the disco ball cast thousands of dots of spinning light over my friends.

Dressed head to toe in silk and feathers, flying above my friends being their silly selves for an audience of fifteen hundred people laughing their faces off, was the best. I giggled out of delight through the rest of the number until my final cue, when I hit the button on the flute and gold, sparkly confetti burst out of the end and fluttered down.

The audience stood and cheered as I descended to the stage floor and the others gathered on either side of me for our bow.

The curtains closed, and Quinn and Jason helped unclip me from the harness and get down off the disco ball. They each locked an elbow with me, their bodies seeming to tremble with the same excitement as mine as we hurried through the door to the dressing room.

Hana rocketed toward us, pulling us all into a group hug. Owen pumped his fists up as he said, "That was freaking amazing. And, Ellie…I mean, aerial stunts, *what?* Awesome."

Through a wry smile, Craig said, "I'm going to be so pissed at you all if this turns me into a theater freak."

Quinn broke us out of our huddle. "You have to get changed for your standup set."

How was I supposed to focus on standup now? On the hilarious topic of cancer? By myself?

I scrambled to get de-feathered, de-gemmed, and de-confettied as the next two acts after ours went up. Quinn, Hana, Owen, and Jason changed out of their costumes and went back to sit in the audience.

I was up next.

The red curtains parted once again.

Alone on center stage, looking out at an endless sea of people, I had only a microphone and a wish I was wearing a gold jumpsuit so I could count on at least one laugh.

But it was just me.

I gripped the mic tight, took a deep breath, and started. "I'll admit I haven't had much experience with dating. So, when I met a cute guy recently, and he tried to kiss me on his porch…"

Because of the stage lights, it was hard to see many faces beyond the third row, but there was Jason in the front, smiling. I had to look away to keep from blushing.

"I was so surprised I stumbled backward down the stairs and got rushed to the hospital…where I found out I have bone cancer. So, yeah, that's my first lesson to you on dating: *don't do it*, because it might lead to *cancer*."

I got a few low rumbling chuckles and a couple awws, but I kept right on going.

"That's right, the *cancer comedy* starts right now, folks." More ripples of laughter.

"People keep telling me, 'Don't eat sugar. Cancer loves sugar. Cancer eats the sugar right up.' And I'm like, 'Really? I love sugar. Cancer and I have a lot in common.'" I smiled like this was a happy coincidence, waited a beat, and then added, "Except, of course, I'm not a leading cause of death."

The audience rewarded me with a bigger laugh, so I pressed on.

"But I took the advice, cut out the sweets, and lost a few pounds. I call it the Cancer Diet. You should try it. It's kind of like Paleo…except you have cancer." I shifted my hands up and down as if weighing the choices.

More laughter.

I adjusted the mic and planted my feet firmly on the stage floor. I went through all the bits Jason and I had come up with about the surgical options, acting out the old lady Beatrice and imagining my sullen ninja donor bone.

The audience was right there with me.

I finished by grabbing a chair and propping my foot up on it, like my leg was on display. Gesturing at my leg, I went into my closing bit, pretending I was on a TV show that fixes beat-up cars. I affected a confident television-host persona, making my voice lower and more deliberate in my delivery, "Ellie's Femur LX is far from blazin' these days. No one's sure how much longer this Femur will ride on, unless the guys at Cancer Customs get on the job, and quick.

"Ellie's jump stick needs to be completely gutted, and the tumors sanded out. Next, the interior will be frozen solid and blasted clean, making the cells cooler than cool. Then the surgeons will use eight-inch chrome rims to fully pimp out the thigh. The other bones on the block are gettin' jealous. *Boo-ya.*"

The audience was eating it up. I delivered my last line like I owned the theater, "Then Ellie's leg will be pimped into a class-A ride."

I strutted around the stage doing a pimp/limp walk.

Laughter soared through the auditorium.

Chapter Twenty-One

Host Tricia Wilson made a big deal about all the Comedy Hub contest judges exiting the auditorium to discuss the winners, and then welcomed Craig and Luke to the stage. "While the judges are making their final decision, we have some local musical talent to entertain you. Please give it up for Craig Kowalski and Luke Rosado of Energy Lab!"

Craig stepped up to the mic at center stage with his amped acoustic guitar as Luke wheeled out a drum set.

I was a little nervous. He was, too, though I was probably the only one who caught the quiet, throat-clicking tic that gave him away. He'd always considered himself a recording artist, and aside from fewer than a handful of coffee-shop gigs and his disco chorus moment, this was his first time on a big stage, in front of hundreds of people, playing his original music.

Once he got set up, made it past a slightly awkward introduction, and started playing his guitar, he relaxed. Craig and Luke's first number was upbeat and sounded nothing at all like the demos I'd heard before. They sounded like a real band. A really *good* band. And Craig's voice was deep, smooth, and resonant. There was character and gravity to the way he sang. Shocked, I turned to Hana and Quinn, who sat riveted in their seats. I willed Jason to get back from the bathroom faster—he needed to see this.

For their third and final song, the stage lights went to black except for one spotlight on Craig. I searched for Jason, hoping he was watching this from the doorway, not wanting to distract people by walking back down to the front row or something.

Hana took my hand and squeezed it as she whispered, "This is what Craig's been working on. He loves you so much."

Craig leaned into the mic and said, "This one is for my sister, Ellie. By the way, you kicked some comedy ass tonight. You'll kick cancer's ass, too." The audience clapped for that, and my eyes welled up. "I have a guest joining me for this song. Please welcome Jason Cooper."

The audience clapped again and another spotlight shone on the microphone stand next to Craig. "What's going on?" I whispered to Quinn and Hana. "Jason hasn't sung since his mom died." They grinned, and this time Quinn reached across and gave my hand a squeeze.

Jason walked into the spotlight, and I almost fell off my chair. He was destined to be a superstar. But then he gave his nervous, one-sided smile, with all the humbleness of the guy who didn't know quite how hot he was, which, of course, automatically made him even more so. *The vicious cycle of humble hotness.*

Craig made a steady beat by slapping his guitar while Jason took the mic, the melody coming only from his voice. He sang slow, low, and soft with only a few notes.

You're in my heart, you're in my head
Rattling around, wish it was me instead
It's a safe place, a wish you well place

A sit back and rest, I need you here space
Wishes swallowed, I hear your voice
Unveil your fears, be your own choice

His voice burrowed into my core. Stunned, my hands pressed at the center of my chest, I breathlessly waited for his next lyrics. Images flooded my mind of our improv moment, our first kiss in the hospital, laughing in rehearsals, him holding me through the night, him fighting for me, despite his loss.

Craig played the guitar—simple, beautiful chords— conjuring up memories of our parents' wedding, my Ice Princess glares, of him being there for me, hugging me close, being my brother every step of the way.

They worked on this together, made this for me. Craig's playing grew louder as they opened up the power of their voices for the chorus, their harmonies filling the expansive auditorium with everything they had.

I can't fix you, but if love could
You are my beacon, you know I would
Travel safely, swiftly along
I will hold you, in my heart and song

You were a stranger, now you're my home
I want to heal you, down to your bones
I want to heal you, down to your bones

I can't fix you, but if love could
You are my beacon, you know I would
Travel safely, swiftly along
I will hold you, in my heart and song

They held the last note, making the sound crescendo until it reverberated through my body. Craig stopped playing the guitar and together they sang-spoke again, quietly, taking a beat between every few words, their harmonies filling up the cracks of heartbreak.

I can't fix you, but if love could
You are my beacon, you know I would

Tears of love and gratitude bubbled and hiccupped out of me, as Craig and Jason bowed their heads. The entire audience was silent. Quinn slipped into the empty chair on the other side of me, and the three of us hugged in our seats, Hana and Quinn's arms wrapped across me, holding on to each other, too. There were sniffles from the people around us, and Quinn's tears ran down my temple. Then someone let out a loud "Woooooo!" and in a wave, the audience was on their feet, clapping and cheering for Craig and Jason, whose faces lit up.

I didn't care that this was a Comedy Hub sponsored show, or whether it was appropriate or not. I rushed to the front of the stage. Craig and Jason kneeled and reached down to hug me. I kissed Craig's cheek and murmured thank-yous into his ear.

Jason jumped off the stage and pulled me to him, one hand around my waist, the other gently on my neck. He leaned in and kissed me in front of the entire audience, our parents, and the Comedy Hub cameras. I kissed him back like it was the only thing that mattered, everything in me combusting and dissolving into the moment, into him, my body capable of this one sort of magic.

Then the audience started chanting, "Do it! Do it! Do it!"

I laughed, but this time I wasn't embarrassed.

If it had been a music contest, Craig would have won. But it wasn't, so Tricia Wilson, her long hair flowing, her white teeth flashing, held the microphone to let us know the winners in each category. "Before I announce the sketch contest winner tonight, I regret to announce that one of the sketch groups was disqualified."

I had a bad feeling about this.

"Unfortunately, since they broke the rule of having no one outside the listed members of the group assist, the sketch 'Las Palomas del Disco' has been disqualified."

There were boos from the audience. The six of us shared a look of shock.

"I'm so sorry, guys. I never would have asked my dads for help with the costumes if I'd known," Quinn said. We all waved off her apology in a flurry of more apologies and questions between us about who read the rules. When we realized none of us had, we tried to smother our laughs.

"I don't actually care that we didn't win," Owen said. "I suspected we might be disqualified for copyright infringement, anyway."

We quietly laughed more as Tricia announced the winning sketch and the members ran up to accept their checks.

"It was never about winning, anyway," Quinn said as she kissed Owen.

Tricia continued. "However, our producer was so entertained by 'Las Palomas del Disco,' that we'll still post it on our site. Congratulations to both groups!"

"*Yes.*" Owen jumped up and punched the air. We all high-fived and hugged, unable to contain our excitement that our sketch would be on one of the most popular sites for funny videos.

At this point, I didn't care who won the standup contest.

Tricia opened up the judges' envelope and said, "And the grand-prize winner in the standup category, who will take home five-hundred dollars and have the recording of tonight's performance aired on ComedyHub.com is…Ellie Hartwood!"

Hana and Quinn jumped up and down by my side, squealing. I stood frozen in disbelief until Jason picked me up and swung me around in the space between the front row and the stage. Someone must have replaced my blood with fancy soda, because my heart was about to bust out of my chest. I guess I did care.

"Hey, get up here, girl! You're our winner." Tricia cheered.

I headed for the stage, my leg aching a bit from all the quick movements I'd forced on it tonight. Tricia handed me the oversize check, and I held it in front of me, thanking her. My face was one big trembling smile as I looked out at the audience cheering for me, and at the row of all the friends I loved most.

I was the luckiest of the unlucky mutants in the world.

Everyone was hugging me and congratulating me when Dad and Barb cut through the crowd toward us, Barb waving her hand. *Dad and Barb made it to the show?*

Dad gave me a huge hug. "I'm so proud of you, Ellie. You took what you're going through and transformed it into something relatable and humorous." Such a Dad way to say *well done*, but it was good to hear.

Barb gave me a kiss on the cheek, her perfume practically knocking me out on the spot. "You sure are one funny lady, Miss Ellie." Ugh. She was trying, but it still hurt not to roll my eyes. Then she said in a quieter, more sincere voice, "I have to say thank you, too." She gulped, and her eyes got watery. "You have been a good influence on my Craigy. That song he sang for you was too beautiful…for…for words. There he is." She wiped her eyes and practically pushed people aside to get to *Craigy,* who was walking down from the sound booth.

Maybe she seemed lame and crazy to me, and maybe I'd never understand her, but the fact she said I was a good influence on Craig had come from a real place. If she hadn't run away so fast, I would have told her it was the other way around.

Dad put his hand on my shoulder. "You leave for New York in the morning?"

"Yep."

"Will you call after your appointment so I know how it went?"

"I will."

"Do. And let me know when you schedule your surgery. I'm going to be there even if you tell me you don't want me there." He smiled and gave me another hug. "Now, I probably need to rescue Craig before Barb squishes him to death."

I laughed. "Go, Dad—*quick.*"

Mom was next, and she swooped me up, hugging me so tight. When she let go, her face glistened with tears. "How did you do that? You amaze me. I'm so lucky to be your mama."

That got me, and the corners of my mouth quivered. She kissed me on the forehead, and I said, "I'm lucky you *are* my mama."

Mom took my hand and was about to say something when Tricia walked up to us. "Ellie, I'm so happy you won. I've only known you for about five minutes, but it feels like longer, and I already love you. Is that too much?" She smiled her golden, camera smile and gave me a huge hug. "I can't wait to see your performance go viral on our site." She winked.

What does that wink mean? I couldn't decide which thing in my life was harder to believe. That I had cancer, that I had Jason, that I'd won the comedy contest, or that this celebrity was saying *she* couldn't wait to see *me* successful. For her, I was probably like a Make-a-Wish kid, and she wanted to make me feel good. It worked.

As Tricia flitted off to talk with the winning sketch group, Jason made a beeline for us.

Mom said to him, "That song made me cry. You have an incredible voice."

His cheeks flushed, and his head dipped. "Thanks, Mrs. Hartwood. I...she..."

Mom saved him by giving him a hug and saying, "You should be very proud of yourself." Then she kissed me on the cheek. "Have fun with your friends, sweetie. I'll see you later tonight. Not too late, okay? We have to leave early in the morning."

When it was just the two of us, he said, "You were amazing up there." He was practically bouncing, giving off this totally amped-up energy.

"That song." I let out a puff of air, having difficulty finding words. "That song, your voice...thank you."

He grinned wide. "Hey, have I ever shown you this grove of trees we have outside the school?"

"A grove of trees? Huh. I'd be very interested in seeing this grove of trees."

He took my hand, and we found our spot in the grass. The leaves that were solid green a month ago were starting to show off their reds and oranges.

Sitting facing each other, we held hands, the energy from the show thrumming between us. I took a deep breath, and the fresh air helped bring me back to earth just a little. Tomorrow, I left for New York.

The words 'carpe diem the crap out of everything' popped into my head. Not romantic words, for sure, but good advice. Jason said he wanted to be with me, and his song made me believe more than ever that his words were true. But no one knew what was next. There was no way I'd expect Jason to stick by me in that kind of unknown. And, if things ended up like a horror movie, there was no way to know if I could handle having him see me like that, or whether I'd be capable of giving anything back.

This was it. Our last time in the grove together. Our last time to be like this with each other for at least a week, maybe for a month or months…possibly forever.

We kissed like we didn't know when we'd kiss again.

I will miss you Jason.

It was a last chance, a prayer, a good-bye…

Good-bye to this boy, good-bye to this body.

Chapter Twenty-Two

As the taxi drove us through Manhattan on Saturday morning, Mom held my hand tight. My heart and gut were speeding and lurching along with the car. Apparently, New York City taxi drivers take the lines on the streets as mere suggestions. What if we came all this way and we didn't like this doctor or his option for surgery? It had already been four weeks since my diagnosis—we couldn't keep pushing out a decision. Despite all that, I was still floating from my good-bye with Jason, and from the fact I'd won the contest and was going to be featured on one of the biggest online comedy sites.

Because that happens all the time.

Staring out the window, I understood all the people who insisted New York City had a different kind of energy. Tall buildings, short buildings, old and new, mashing up against each other yet still regal and impressive. I peered into windows when traffic slowed, and imagined all the dreams and worries and goings-on behind the glass. Dancers, bankers, bakers, writers, people on the corner selling purses from a cart…

Why would anyone buy a purse from a cart? So weird.

The taxi dropped us off where we'd be staying during our visit—in a condo belonging to the Synnestvedt family, friends of the Coopers who were out of the country on business for the year.

It was a majestic building on the Upper East Side, directly across from Central Park. Mom and I got out and—jaw drop—right across the street was the Guggenheim, the modern art museum with the funky, circular exterior.

When we walked up to the condo, a doorman took our bags and said, "You must be the Hartwoods? Welcome." He ushered Mom and me inside, telling us more about the building and the Synnestvedts' wishes for us to make ourselves at home. Neither Mom nor I could speak. The doorman passed us off to the elevator operator, who was also friendly.

The hit-the-jackpot feeling blossomed when we opened the door to what would be our home for the next two nights: a three-bedroom penthouse with a sprawling brick patio with a view of the park.

"Ooh, French doors. I love French doors." I unlocked them. Nothing like our flimsy, sticky, sliding-glass door at home. The air was a touch cooler up here than it was on street level. Mom and I walked out onto the patio. Beyond the rail, the Central Park treetops were tipped with bright red, orange, and yellow.

"This is nuts. You really met the right people this year, honey." Mom goaded me with a little elbow jab to my side.

"I mean, when Mr. Cooper said he had friends with a place near the hospital, I never thought he meant a freaking palace on the Park. This is out of control." I pressed a switch on the side of the wall, and fairy lights came sparkling on along the rail and in the flowerpots. Magical.

"I don't know how we'll ever thank the Coopers and the Synnestvedts for their generosity," Mom said.

"It's pretty much impossible. But I know they like helping

us, too, so at least it's not a total loss on their part, right?"

"That's right, sweetie." She kissed my forehead. "And you don't need to worry about it, because this was meant to be. When truly bad things happen, the fates conspire to help those in need, don't they?" Considering homelessness, famine, and war, Mom's theory didn't hold, but I wasn't going to question the beauty of all the support I was receiving.

We went back inside talking in our best snooty accents and flitting around deciding who would sleep in which room and requesting things of our imaginary butler.

I dreamed I was on a hospital table. A smiling doctor put his hands over my leg. There were bright orbs of light all around me, filling the room, overwhelming me with a sense of peace. Where the doctor held my leg, I saw my femur bone inside me glow a radiant white. Clean.

With a gasp I awoke, my eyes widening to the darkness of my bedroom, a light buzz surging through my body, like my physical form might float away and dissipate from the bed any second. A smile came over me. I didn't dare move, not wanting to disturb the peaceful image from the dream, or shake the sensation. I was brimming with this abstract knowingness. Closing my eyes again, I took a mental snapshot of the dream image and the feeling of seeing my femur glow, clean and cured.

I lay there in that state for what could have been minutes or hours before I fell back asleep. Whatever the time was, I made a wish that the transformation would stay with me.

On Monday morning, Mom and I sat in Dr. Ray's waiting room for six hours. Seriously. Six. Mom paced the room back and forth in the same line, while flipping through a magazine, never pausing long enough to see the pages. I reread the article "Top Ten Miracle Surgeons" that featured Dr. Ray, praying he could work a miracle for my case.

When we finally got into the exam room, I put on the familiar gown—they were all the same—and we proceeded to wait for another hour. Mom was huffing and puffing, saying things like, "Well, no matter what his opinion is, no patient deserves to be treated like this." I tried to keep her focused on her magazines. I weighed myself. Played with the buttons on the examining table/chair thingy. Tried to imagine myself as Chief of Oncology. It didn't seem very fun.

Dr. Ray finally entered. He was rosy cheeked and wore a red bow-tie and said a warm, "Hello." Despite him making us wait for hours, I had a good feeling about him. He put my scans up and stated all the options, and when I asked his opinion, he explained it in detail.

"Your case is unique. You don't really see a tumor of this length and magnitude."

I'm so special.

"We have to consider your age, and the size of your tumor. We are going to have to improvise a little here." He won major points for saying "improvise." "Since it is so long, it would be difficult to get a donor bone that would be the right size and match for your leg. The problem with going with a total titanium replacement is that it eventually wears out. Not exactly desirable for a seventeen-year-old, eh?"

Mom and I shook our heads. Mom said, "Dr. Nichols recommended amputation. She said it would give Ellie more mobility and a better chance of"—Mom shifted in her seat—"survival and keeping the cancer from coming back."

His mouth became a firm line as he considered this. "With my idea, we can avoid the numerous complications of amputation and achieve the same low probabilities of risk."

Mom gripped my hand, and tears pricked with the relief that I might be able to keep my beautiful leg.

"I want to save your bone. What I'm suggesting is unorthodox. I want to treat it with cryosurgery, where we freeze the bone to such a degree that all the cancer cells are killed off. Then we would put the bone back into your body, using a titanium plate to secure it as it revascularizes. Do you know what that means?"

"Yes, where the marrow of the bone comes back." I was glad I'd studied.

"Right. Basically, it becomes alive again instead of sitting there in your leg, a dead thing. I like this option for you because, like I said, finding an acceptable donor bone for you would be difficult. However, another tricky thing with your case is that your bone is so bowed." With his index finger, he followed the swooping curve of my bone on the scan. "I'd have a titanium plate created that would run along the outside of your femur to support it while the bone gets a chance at revascularization. The downsides are there are a lot of variables to this surgery, and it would require keeping weight off your leg for a full year."

"You mean, Ellie would be on crutches for a year?" Mom asked.

"Assisted walking, yes. Mostly crutches."

This was crazy.

A year.

Would my shoulders survive?

"What about being able to fully bend and straighten my leg again?" I asked.

He sighed. "I'm going to be honest with you. It's not likely with any of these surgeries. There is a high probability you will have long-term challenges with your gait—a limp. You won't be able to run or jump for many years, maybe ever. There are state-of-the-art prosthetics, and if you were a competitive athlete we might reevaluate that option, but I get the sense from what I've learned about you and your interests, that keeping your leg is best for you."

My insides buckled. This was supposed to be my miracle surgeon. I'd hoped for something better, more reassuring. But he agreed that even with the best outcome I'd never have a fully functioning leg again.

Mom put her arms around me as I covered my face in my hands and took deep breaths. The pressure against my forehead and cheekbones steadied me, and my dark, mini cavern of air gave me a moment to process this. *I have cancer, it's in me, and I need it out so I can fight for my life.*

I slid my hands back down and focused my eyes on Dr. Ray's, like I could see into him, into his abilities, into the future. He didn't rush me. He simply smiled and held my gaze until my heartbeat calmed and I knew. Despite the fact I was signing up for an unorthodox surgery with no guarantee other than that I'd be on crutches for a year, I was certain—absolutely, 100 percent in-my-gut-and-heart certain—that he was the doctor for me.

Chapter Twenty-Three

Just call me Princess Cancerella.

Aside from the whole cancer thing, I couldn't believe how lucky I was. Because it was the Saturday night after my appointment with Dr. Ray, and Hana and Quinn were here with me. In a penthouse. In New York City. If I could have suspended the life-changing reality of my surgery looming before me, this was like a fairytale. And I was the princess. Except regular princesses never seem to have cancer, just the common mishaps with all the wicked witches and stepmothers and evil poisons disguising themselves as edible foodstuffs and so forth.

My surgery was scheduled for Monday. Dr. Ray had moved everything around to get me in so fast, and Mom made an arrangement with the school for me to do the work I could from afar. She also sorted out staying as long as we needed in the Synnestvedts' place.

Everything had come together, but I was still freaked knowing that soon my left leg would be sliced from knee to hip, my femur bone temporarily removed from my body, and my life forever altered.

My stomach twisted for the eleventy-billionth time.

Thanks to Quinn's mom's surplus of frequent flyer miles from all her international travel, she flew Quinn and Hana to New York City for my farewell-to-walking-for-a-year weekend.

Even Craig, my dad, and Barb had flown out yesterday. Craig stayed with us at the penthouse, and Barb and Dad at a hotel close to the hospital where I'd have surgery.

I had a feeling after this little stint I'd be writing thank-you notes to people until I was twenty.

If only Jason could be here.

Don't get greedy, Ellie.

After adventuring through Manhattan, we finished the day with some shopping. Mostly I got hospital necessities, but we splurged on one nice outfit for tonight, too. It was Mom's treat for me because Quinn, Hana, Craig and I had a big evening out ahead of us, including plans to see a live improv show at the place I'd always dreamed of going: the Upright Citizens Brigade Theater.

My friends and I were in our bras and the bottom halves of our outfits, doing our hair and makeup in the master bathroom, where the walls were covered in a meticulous mosaic of shiny tiles.

"No wonder you're all strong and muscley—that looks like a workout," Hana said, looking into the bathroom mirror at me as I flat-ironed her hair.

"I know. My vanity makes me strong, gives me guns." I smiled at her reflection and flexed my biceps. "It's got nothing to do with walking around on crutches for a month."

"That's what I figured." Hana nodded.

I finished straightening her hair and smoothing some shine-cream through the ends. "You look gorgeous." I'd never seen this sleeker side. What I'd done made her black hair look even more dramatic against her smooth skin.

The door swung open. "Hey, are you three—" It was Craig. "Hey, awesome. I hope that's what you all are wearing tonight, because that's hot."

"Craig!" We all shouted at him in unison as we covered our tops. Quinn dashed across the bathroom, growled at Craig, and slammed the door.

I couldn't resist. "Ugh—*brothers*."

We decided it would be wise to take a break from makeup and hair to finish getting dressed. Hana traded in one of her signature cute-things-in-nature T-shirts for a red top and a layered necklace Quinn loaned her. She looked older. I started to tear up thinking how I'd most likely be losing her to New York City for good next year. "I'm so excited to visit you when you live here."

"Slow down there, Captain Pretender. Let's focus on step one: get accepted to NYU."

"You'll get in, Hana, I just know it," Quinn said as she swiped on another layer of lip-gloss and admired herself in the mirror. She'd gone for an eclectic look, with tights and a short skirt, mixing bright colors and multiple accessories in a way only she could.

I pulled on my new, low-cut blouse over my shiny black jeans.

"That color blue really brings out your eyes," Quinn said.

I smiled at the three of us in the mirror. We might pass as people who belonged in New York City. "Do you two think I was crazy to waste good money on an outfit I won't be able to wear again anytime soon?" My leg would be super puffy post-surgery, so these tight new jeans wouldn't fit for a while.

"Don't be silly, Ellie." Quinn came up and side-hugged me. "Think of it this way. You won't be going to homecoming or probably prom, so this outfit is a steal compared to those dresses." After the words spilled out of her mouth, we all froze for a second. My mood sank. I'd realized homecoming was out, but the thought of not being able to dance at prom because I'd still be on crutches made the rest of my senior year sound bleak. Quinn pulled away to look at me, biting her lip, eyes wide.

"Don't worry, Quinn. I wasn't exactly excited about prom. I mean, Hana and I spent last year's dance watching a Harry Potter marathon, so you know formal school functions aren't on the top of my list. I just sometimes get these little shockwaves over what I won't be able to do."

"Hey. If you decide you *do* want to go to prom, we'll just have Gary and Steven pull out the bird dress and ol' disco ball, and you can hover above it all," Hana said. "That'd be way better than having to support your own weight the whole night anyway. I mean, that crap's exhausting."

"Huh. That sounds…frightening." I laughed, losing the flash of sullenness as quickly as it came.

"Ooh. Dancing. We need to go dancing after the show tonight." Quinn clapped her hands together.

"What?" Hana and I asked.

"What better way to spend the eve of the eve of your surgery than shakin' like crazy? Or gently swaying on the surgery leg, but shakin' everything else." One leg firmly planted, she demonstrated shimmying the rest of her body.

I laughed.

"Yes, let's," Hana said, mimicking the inflection we used in our improv warm-up that required everyone to respond with "Yes, let's!" to any suggestion anyone shouted out.

The doorbell rang. Wondering who that could be, I cocked my head at Quinn and Hana, whose faces had transformed—Quinn's now had a teeth-baring grin, and Hana's features had shifted to *mischievous*.

Jason.

He stood in the doorway looking taller, handsomer, and smilier than ever. I couldn't help it: I squealed and sprang toward him. He hugged me tight and said, "Surprise!"

When we calmed down enough for him to set me back down, I sputtered questions at him. "What are you doing here? How? When? Are you here alone?"

"Dad's downstairs finishing up a call right now, but he'll be up in a second. I gave him a multi-layered pitch for why we should come to New York right now, but my main point was that I would hold it against him for a lifetime if he didn't let me fly out here for this."

"Ah, yes, that would be convincing." I smiled, heat spreading across my cheeks.

Jason flew to New York City to see me.

We'd just finished watching the most awesome improv show at the Upright Citizens Brigade Theater, and then froze our butts off getting to a club that was having an under-twenty-one night. There'd been a cold snap in the city, and we hadn't brought jackets, so we were all happy to be dancing in the heat of the club.

"I mean, that show makes you embarrassed you ever tried improv," Quinn said as she flitted and swayed around. "And scared to ever try it again because you know it won't even orbit the same universe of brilliance and hilariousness."

"Or, it makes you want to immediately move here and sign up for every single improv class and go to every single show possible," Hana shouted over the music. "If I don't get into NYU, I'm gonna freak." She froze mid-spin, a guilty look on her face. "I'm so sorry, Ellie."

"Stop it. Just because we don't know if I'll be in any

condition to go to college next fall, doesn't mean I can't be excited for you. It can't be about The Leg all the time."

Jason and Craig came back with some bottled waters for us. I stopped in my dance-tracks to stare at Jason. He'd taken off his long-sleeved shirt and was wearing a tight-fitting white tee. His hair was sweaty and unruly, and he ran his hand through it, making it stick up even more. *He flew here to surprise me.*

"Hi."

"Hi."

We stared at each other stupidly.

He took a big inhale. "So, yeah. Wow. Have I mentioned you look totally amazing?"

He had. Repeatedly. He leaned in and kissed my neck lightly, causing little flares to leap around my pores like whack-a-moles.

The music transitioned to the next song, one we all knew, and the moment between Jason and me gave way to all of us bopping up and down—me not actually lifting my feet off the ground, since no jumping was allowed—and taking turns singing out loud.

We were all cheesing it up big-time. Even Craig was swaying side to side a bit, as Hana circled him in a dancing fury. It went back to the chorus, and we formed a circle of karaoke-dance-off abandon.

Craig picked up Hana. She wrapped her legs easily around his waist as he spun them around, their smiles so radiant I imagined teeny lightning bolts zapping between them.

Jason tugged on my hand, pulling me close. I nuzzled into him, resting my head on his shoulder. *More of this. But without the loud music and the standing.* "Do you want to go?" I asked. He nodded, and I tapped on Quinn's shoulder. "Hey, are you guys cool if we take off early and meet you back at the penthouse later?"

"Never let it be said I was a nookie-thwarter. Go. Go," Quinn said.

"There will be no nookie," I mouthed back at her.

By the time the cab pulled up in front of the apartment building at 5th Ave and 88th Street, there was already a thin sheen of snow covering the city, frosting it clean and new. We exited on the Central Park side of the street, and I imagined scaling the brick wall that surrounded the park and skipping through the moonlit night batting at the million puffy flakes.

"I can't believe it's snowing," Jason said.

"Our global climate crisis's little gift to us." I twirled around once—because I could—as snowflakes fell thick and wet on my lashes. "I love it."

"Me, too." With his snow-drenched eyelashes, he leaned in and gave me butterfly kisses.

"I wish there was enough for a snowball fight." But it wasn't sticking to the ground.

"I'd totally win."

"No way. My snow ammo would fly so fast and furious, I'd *bury* you in snowballs."

"You think so, huh?"

"I know so."

"Get ready to be proven wrong." He reached down and pretended to scoop up a pile of snow and mash it into a ball.

"Really? A mime snowball fight? How improv-nerdy are we willing to get here?"

"Full-on. You've been warned." He pulled his arm back and launched the air-ball at me.

Despite its nonexistence, I yelped and ducked, shaping my own fake snowball low to the ground and then flinging it at Jason.

He acted like it was a direct hit, jolting back, his hand to his chest. "Argh!"

I pretended to pull on a utility belt and pack to hold my snow-ammo and then formed snowball figments at warp speed, complete with sound effects. "*Shhik. Whoom. Ch-kunk.*"

Not to be outdone, he built an ice fortress with cannons.

"Oh, it's going to be like that, is it?" I granted myself magic powers, conjured my inner Elsa, and created an even bigger ice fortress. Then our battle really began. We were shooting and flinging, recoiling and rolling (me in slow-mo to protect my leg) all along the patch of grass between the park's brick wall and 5th Ave. We ignored the looks from strangers and played and laughed until we crumpled to the ground.

When our laughs simmered to light giggles, and I'd caught my breath, I said, "I won."

"Uh, no way. I had *catapults*."

"Clunky and old-school. Didn't you see how my ice lasers demolished your entire weapons stash?"

"What? No, they did not."

I *tsked*. "Ah-ah—no denials."

"Well, you must have denied my storm shields that blocked your lasers."

"You're making that up just now, or you made them up when I wasn't looking. There were no storm shields."

He grumbled and tickled me until I giggled again. "Those were pretty awesome ice lasers," he finally admitted as I pushed his hands away.

"Thank you." The snowy leaves arching over from the park sparkled with the reflections of the streetlights. "I feel so alive, you know?" The words came out quietly, causing a weird traffic jam in my throat.

He held my hand and gave a small smile. "I do." He leaned his head back onto the cold ground and closed his eyes. I did the same, reaching my chin toward the night sky, the snowflakes pattering against my face.

"Every first snowfall of the season, my mom would say 'put your face toward heaven so you can receive all the angel kisses.'"

"I like that. She was a good mom."

"The best."

I imagined each soft droplet was a connection from somewhere, something beyond my understanding, showering love and reassurances down on us. I wondered if Jason was thinking about his mom's angel surrounding him tonight.

"Okay, I'm freezing now," Jason said, jumping up and reaching down to pull me up by the hand.

We bought two cups of hot cocoa at a corner store and took them back to our building. Tiptoeing inside the dark penthouse holding hands, we shushed each other so we wouldn't wake our parents. The room I was now staying in was a tiny thing off the kitchen, about the size of a large walk-in closet. The bigger room I'd been sleeping in for the last week I'd given over to Jason's dad. Mom was in the master bedroom, and Quinn and Hana were sharing the bunk-bed room. Craig and Jason had been relegated to the couches.

Jason grabbed the comforter off my bed, and we took it and our cocoa outside to the patio. We sat on a bench and wrapped ourselves up in the blanket. We still had the snow and the view and the night and each other, but now with zero probability of frostbite.

When we finished our drinks, he pulled me onto his lap and kissed me. His hand brushed along my back and the sides of my waist.

"Your body is incredible," he said.

I frowned. "Except for one thing."

"No. Your body is incredible, and it's getting ready to evict that squatter for good."

It was. It would.

I cupped his face and kissed him back, tearing up that I even got the chance to love him. In this world, there was nothing to fear about that.

"I love you, Jason."

His smile filled my hands. "I love you, Ellie."

His words filled my bones. He was my lucky star in this maelstrom of misfortune. I wondered how it was possible that my life was at its very best and its very worst simultaneously. Messy and beautiful. Heartbreaking and inspiring.

Chapter Twenty-Four

'Twas the night before Surgery, when all through the penthouse...

It was Surgery Eve. Mom, Mr. Cooper, Quinn, Hana, Craig, Jason, and I were gathered in a circle in front of the gas fireplace in the living room. We'd all gone out to dinner, with Barb and Dad, too, though they were now back at their hotel for the night. Surprisingly, it wasn't as weird as I would have imagined having Mom, Dad, and Barb eating together at the same table. I guess cancer really puts people on their best behavior.

Two points for cancer?

The little lights of the big city twinkled through the windows. I wondered how many other people like me were out there, people knowingly on the verge of everything changing. How many surgeries were scheduled every day? How many people would wake up the next morning and learn their lives had been flipped upside-down for good or bad? And what about the other people? Those whose lives wouldn't significantly change tomorrow, people simply sitting in front of the TV, waiting to get up for another ordinary day, never even considering how incredibly awesome their legs were.

Everyone in our circle was in their pajamas, except me. I wore a pair of shorts and a sweatshirt Quinn and Hana had made for me. On the front, it had a cartoon version of the three of us holding hands, each with a different cute animal on our heads—a bunny, a bird, and a hedgehog. So cute.

"Okay, Hana, you're a talented artist, I think you should start," Mom instructed, handing Hana a green marker and pointing to my leg.

On my left thigh, Hana drew a funny, smiley femur-bone character doing a happy jig.

Quinn took a red marker and added a big heart on my leg, writing inside the heart the words: *We love you, Dr. Ray.*

"Ah, that tickles," I said, as the marker made smooth wet loops on my leg. I hoped Dr. Ray would at least get a smile out of all the messages to him, and not be annoyed by the visuals on his surgery site.

Craig leaned over to my right leg. He drew a big X on my thigh and then wrote in big block letters: NOT THIS LEG. We all laughed. Mom took the red marker and added, *Take extra special care of this one,* and drew smiley faces and stars all around it.

Mr. Cooper took a blue marker to my calf and drew a little sailboat with words trailing behind like waves that read, *Bon voyage, cancer.*

"Good one, Michael." Mom patted him on the back. He smiled at her. It was quick, but I caught it—their eyes sharing this moment of understanding. I had to turn away, not wanting to think too much more about what it must be like for them.

Jason grabbed the black marker. He covered his work with his other hand as he drew for a while. "What are you putting on there that's so involved?" I asked.

"Wait for it." He switched to the red marker, then green, then blue, adding more and more. "There." He finally finished and revealed his handiwork. He'd written, *Pimp my leg,* in funky letters with a picture of a leg with all these added gadgets—tires, speakers, springs, and a bucket labeled MAGIC HEALING DUST.

I loved it and gave Jason a smile saying so.

Mom covertly wiped away a tear as she put the markers away. Then she put a too-big smile on her face and clapped her hands together. "I have an idea. Let's all put a hand on Ellie's leg and one by one say a prayer, or something we wish for her."

I sucked in air. *Don't know about that.* But I wasn't in the place for objections so I stayed silent.

Hana turned off the overhead lights so that only the firelight was around us. They all inched in closer to me, placing their hands on my legs. A rush of warmth whirled through my body.

Mr. Cooper started. "Ellie, I'm so thankful for the happiness you've brought to my son's life. I'm proud of how you're handling your battle." I smiled at him. He was so kind to be here. "I wish you a speedy and full recovery."

I bit the inside of my cheeks and stretched my eyes wide to keep them dry. *They are turning me into mush. An extremely-well-loved pile of mush.*

Quinn was next in the circle. "I pray you kick some cancer ass tomorrow. You are my hero, and I love you so much." She kissed me on the cheek.

Craig took a moment to think, then looked at me. "Hands down, the best thing that came out of my mom remarrying and abandoning me is you. I'm thankful to call you sister, and that you'll finally *let* me call you that without hitting me or yelling at me." I laughed. "I need you to heal up fast so you can get back to sharing cereal and anime with me, and letting me torture you with my music."

My eyes were a glassy haze of tears now. I leaned in and gave Craig a kiss on the cheek and whispered, "Thanks, bro. I'll do my best for you." I wiped my face with the cuffs of my new sweatshirt.

Hana was next. She held my hand and looked straight into my eyes. "Ellie, I've really admired your calm these last few days. I would say I pray for you to heal well and for everything to go smoothly tomorrow, but I don't need to pray. I just *know*. I know you will defeat the odds." She dropped my hand and gave me a huge, gripping hug.

The love around me blazed warmer than the fire. A determined part of me believed this darkness and pain and cancer couldn't possibly stand a chance against the force of my family and friends.

Jason put his hands on my legs and leaned in, speaking quietly. "I am so thankful I walked onto that stage and into that scene with you." I made a face, thinking of our start together. "Seriously, Ellie. Um…" He paused and took a deep breath. "You think this cancer has been a burden on everyone, but for me… it's been…" He trailed off. Took another breath. "I'm not feeling as eloquent as everyone else." He held my hand. "I'm just looking forward to when you're onstage again, or on your bicycle, shocking all the doctors with your mad rotation skills like you never had titanium plates in your leg." He leaned in even closer and gave me a melty, wonderful kiss.

Everyone whistled or awwed for a second.

Jason sat back in his spot in the circle, and I let out a quiet laugh. I hoped they were right in their optimism, but I was still scared. The reality was that even with one of the top surgeons in the country, this procedure had only been done five times—and that was only counting procedures *similar* to this one. Counting procedures exactly like mine, I'd be the first.

I remembered what Gary said about fearlessness not being the absence of fear, but going forward, anyway. I wanted to say something poetic and meaningful back. To tell them each how grateful I was and how much they meant to me, but all I was able to get out was a shaky "thank you."

Mom put her hand on my shoulder. "You are the light of my life, sweet Ellie. Know that all your guardian angels will be by your side tomorrow, okay?" Her breath was uneven and she was having trouble getting the words out. "I know you will get through this and soon be on to all the big, beautiful things that await you in this life."

Closing my eyes, I tried to make an imprint of this moment in my mind. Hopes, fears, they didn't matter—I was ready to face tomorrow.

Chapter Twenty-Five

I woke up. A bright light flooded my vision. It was hard to see.

Squinting my eyes, I turned my head, trying to look past the light. The room had changed.

"Ellie? Ellie, sweetie, are you awake?" It was Mom.

"Ellie? Hi. Are you okay? Do you need the nurse?" That was Jason. "She's so…so puffy, Mrs. Hartwood. You can hardly recognize her."

"It's all the fluid, Jason. Ellie? Can you hear us?"

I still couldn't see them—just a bright, blurry white. I tried harder to focus, but it wasn't their faces I saw.

It was the woman from the portrait in Jason's house. His mom. Linda Cooper.

She was beautiful, glowing, and smiling. I tried to reach out. Her presence emanated warmth and happiness. She spoke, the words not quite making sense yet, and pointed to another light, where there were two figures, one small and one tall. I didn't understand, but the vision made me feel at peace. I closed my eyes again.

"It might take a while before she fully comes to." It

sounded like my dad, but was far away.

"I guess she still needs to sleep." Mom's voice. I strained to see her. My eyelids were too heavy.

Wake up. Wake up.

This time I opened my eyes and Linda's face faded back as the outline of Jason's face emerged out of her light.

"Jason," I whispered. "Your mom's here."

"What? Yes, your mom's right here," Jason said, not understanding me.

Mom's hand gripped mine. "Hi, sweetie. You did such an incredible job."

"Hi, Mom." It was hard to get the words out. "Jason's mom—Linda. Jason…she's here…she's with you when you need her."

It went dark again.

The next time I woke up I didn't feel as out of it. I was able to open my eyes fully without the lids automatically wanting to fall shut. I didn't know how much longer it had been, but there were Jason and Mom in the corner of the room, reading books.

"Hi," I managed.

They popped their heads up and came to my bedside.

"How are you feeling now?" Mom asked.

"Pain. My leg's throbbing."

"Here, hit this morphine button." Mom put the cord in my hand.

"Thanks."

Jason's brows were furrowed, and I could tell he was biting his cheeks.

"Are you scared of me? Do I look awful?"

"You do look a little like the Michelin Man," Mom said,

patting my hand. Leave it to Mom to not hold back. I gave a weak smile.

"Are you hungry? Thirsty?" Jason asked.

"Not hungry. Very thirsty. And itchy."

"I'll have the nurse add Benadryl to your IV," Mom said and went out of the room to hunt for the nurse.

"I'm glad you're here." I glimpsed Jason through squinted eyes. I did feel supremely puffy.

"The others are in the café snacking it up." Jason smiled his side-of-the-mouth smile. Kissing him sounded nice, but I was certain my lips wouldn't have cooperated, being that they were dry and bloated and lacking muscles.

"Do I really look like the Michelin Man?"

"Well, because of the slight green tone, I'd say more like a mini Incredible Hulk—a Hulkette." He waited a beat. "It was scary for a while. You needed a couple blood transfusions. I'm just happy to see you're awake and not talking about bright lights or my mom. I thought you were, um, crossing over or something." He pulled my blanket up a little higher around my shoulders. "Do you think it was a dream, or did you... really see..."

"Your mom?"

He nodded.

"It felt way more real than a dream is all I can say. Her presence was with me." The knowledge swept over me like a huge comfort.

Tears brimmed his eyes.

"Jason, she loves you so much. She's with you more than you know, and she's proud of the person you've become." The words just came out as if they were facts I knew by heart, not simply because they sounded nice. Jason dropped his head and a tear fell onto the bed.

"I miss her every single day." He paused. "I'm so glad you're okay. I'm glad she was watching over you through all of this." He kissed my hand.

I couldn't do much, but I squeezed his hand and tried to remember the details of the dream so I could tell it to him when I was more with it.

"Are you still feeling any pain in your leg?" Jason asked as he dried his eyes on a tissue.

I gave a breathy laugh. "You'd make a good doctor." I hadn't seen my leg yet. I reached down to grab the edge of the white sheet, and pulled it aside.

Oh my God.

My left leg was two or three times the size of my right leg, and in shades of green, yellow, and purple that made me think of regurgitated Easter eggs. Thick, black stitches poked up fiercely all along the outside of my leg from knee to hip. Mom walked into the room as I examined it.

"Did Tim Burton do the stitch-up job?" I asked, gasping at the monstrosity that was once a normal leg. "Did they get it all out? Is it going to be okay?"

Mom came around the other side of the bed and took my non-IV-burdened hand. "It went extremely well. You were in there for ten hours, but they got all the tumor cells out.

"The extra good news is he was able to save all the ligaments in your knee. That means you have an even better chance than expected of regaining rotation," Mom said.

That did make me feel better.

Jason handed me a cup of water. "And the titanium plate fit just right."

"That's a lot to take in right now, sweetie. Dr. Ray will stop by early in the morning to check on you," Mom said.

"Who sent all these flowers?" Bouquets and cards covered the windowsill, dresser, and bedside table.

"Everyone." Mom smiled. "We can read all the cards that came with them when you have more energy."

There was a tap on the door, and then it opened. "Ellie-bee, you're awake."

"Dad."

"You did it, kiddo." He kissed my forehead then gave me a large wrapped box.

I unwrapped it to reveal several pairs of the softest pajamas. "Thanks, Dad. Just what I'll need."

"There's a card somewhere in there, too." He rifled around in the box till he found it under some tissue paper and handed it to me.

It read:

I love you with all my heart. Keep healing strong. Love, Dad

"Thanks, Dad. I love you, too."

Mom said, "Very thoughtful, Frank." They shared the first genuine smile between them I'd witnessed in years.

There were more knocks on the door. "Can we come in?" Quinn asked, Hana and Craig by her side.

"Of course," Mom said, waving them in, the room now cramped. "Frank, why don't we take a walk and give the kids some time. It'll give us a chance to talk about a few logistics."

Hana, Quinn, and Craig gave me hugs, cooed at me, told me how scared they'd been, how happy they were to see me. I showed them my leg, and they cringed, covered their mouths, and generally didn't hold back their flinching terror. *Comforting.*

"Guess what?" Quinn said to me, handing me her phone.

"What?"

"We're getting a tiny bit internet famous," Hana said, clicking play on the cued-up video of our Las Palomas del Disco sketch on Comedy Hub's website. "It posted this morning."

"What?" I jolted up a fraction in surprise, but even that small movement caused a pang, so I eased back down, holding still as I watched in disbelief. There were already thousands of likes.

"Hana, these comments. They all love you."

She blushed and clicked around to another video. "Wait until you see this one. Someone from the audience posted it over the weekend." It was a video of Craig and Jason singing.

I gasped. "You guys. Your song. I bet that recording deal isn't far away now, Craig."

"We'll see," he said, but his face radiated hope.

"It's not all good news for us," Hana said. She showed me the comments from all the people losing their minds over Craig and Jason. Some of the comments were extremely blunt about what they wished to do with our boyfriends.

"Whoa. Wow. Please never read these, Jason."

"Too late." It was his turn to blush.

"Enough of that. This one is even better," Craig said. He clicked play on the video of my standup set. It was surreal seeing myself onstage under the spotlight, energetic and confident. Especially now, being in this hospital bed, a puffy, stitched-up, immobile green thing.

"Read the comments," Quinn said, scrolling down on the phone.

Comedy Hub had subtitled the post with an announcement to the world that I was getting my surgery today and asking everyone to wish me well. People were sharing it. There were hundreds of comments.

Praying for you.
You're so funny. You rock. Get well soon.
Sending big love and prayers.
You're an inspiration.
You got this.
We love you, Ellie Hartwood.

It hit me hard and fast. Strangers. All over the world. Praying for *me*. Sending me their love. My shoulders shook and tears slid down my face.

There was a longer comment toward the bottom.

My son was recently diagnosed. We've been so devastated. This is our first laugh since. Thank you. Please give us an update of your surgery. Hugs.

My heart ached and swelled, my world expanding.

"And, the best for last." Quinn played a fourth video.

There, in my hand, on this phone, via the internet, where the world could access it forever, were Jason and me kissing in front of the Porter stage to the booming "do it" chants.

"Oh…no. Oh God." I covered my face. "Someone please hit that morphine button a few billion times for me real quick."

I woke up again later, and this time it was just Jason with me. He put his book down and lifted a package out from behind a chair in the corner of the room and brought it to me.

I pulled back layers of bubble wrap and uncovered the gift. A framed painting. It looked mostly like a realistic cross section of a thigh that might be found in an anatomy textbook. But in the middle, instead of only a bone, there was this wonderland of flowers—in purples, blues, and greens—growing out of the center of the bone with rays of gleaming light.

There were no adequate words for how happy seeing this strong, beautiful bone made me feel, and how loved, knowing Jason must have put hours into it. But I tried. "This means the world to me. It's stunning."

"Well, you know, when you're up worrying night after night, it's more fun to paint than stare at the ceiling."

"You were worried about me?"

He nodded. "Of course."

"You climbed through my window. You wrote me a song and sang it in front of an entire audience. You flew out to New York to be with me. You made me this gorgeous painting. I'm getting the feeling you plan on sticking around."

He laughed. "Have I been too subtle?"

"I plan on sticking around, too."

I smiled and propped his painting up at the end of my bed so my body would be inspired to grow and heal like the flowers blooming from the bone.

Epilogue

Ten months later

It's a warm August night on the Boulder campus, a soft breeze blowing as we settle onto the stone benches in the beautiful outdoor theater. Our semester just started, and CU's improv group is about to begin their first show of the season. My belly flutters with anticipation. Auditions are next week, and this could be my new improv group someday soon. Correction: it could be *our* new improv group—Jason decided to go to CU, too. There are the mountains I've been waiting for on my right, and the boy I've always wanted on my left.

Perfect.

Jason kisses me sweetly on the lips and takes my crutches, tucking them behind our legs on the ground. Yes, ten months clomping around on these metal flanks. So, not everything is perfect. But I try not to complain. Mostly I just feel lucky, and I only have two more months to go before I'm crutch-free.

I had my nine-month follow-up appointment with Dr. Ray before Jason and I packed up our stuff and caravanned from Illinois to Colorado with our parents to move into both our dorms. Quinn is off traveling the world, but Hana and Craig are both living in New York City now and were with me at the appointment. Dr. Ray looked impressed when he asked me to lie on my stomach, reach back for my ankle, and pull my heel toward my butt to see how much rotation I'd regained in my knee. I was only three inches away from touching—way above their estimate of what I'd ever get back—and I'm determined to get to 100 percent.

Using the exercises Mrs. Lahiri and my physical therapist taught me, I get up every morning without fail to lie on my stomach on the floor with an icepack tucked under my lower thigh, just above my knee. I reach back and pull my ankle in as far as I can, to the threshold of pain, and hold it there, trying to breath instead of grimace. I push it a centimeter further for as many seconds as I can tolerate, and then flip over to do my quad isometrics, which are as boring as they sound.

As the show starts, Jason leans over and whispers, "I can't wait to do improv with you up there someday."

"I wish I didn't have to audition with crutches. They make all my characters, you know, so crutchy all the time."

"Just remember the second Mash-Up. If you perform like that, they'll want to switch their form to crutch-prov."

I kiss him on the cheek, and he puts his arm around me, pulling me even closer to him. Everything in me is warm and glowy. I still can't believe he chose Boulder over all his other choices. He promised it was because of their experimental film program. But also, when I argued with him about his choice, he said, "Plus, Mom told me to always follow my heart. To follow love."

What gets me even more was he made that choice during the most grueling, early months of my recovery, when I was stuck in bed, foggy from painkillers, with my leg in a passive motion machine for sixteen hours a day. I still don't think my pushing him away and giving him a chance to get out while he could was wrong, but I'm grateful every day that he chose to stay. Because my miracle doctor lived up to his title, and now we're here on the other side of cancer, on one of the most idyllic campuses in the country, about to watch what is sure to be some awesome improv.

Except…

As we crutch/walk from the theater after the show, across the quad and away from the crowd, Jason breaks our stunned silence by saying, "Wow. That was really, really…"

"Terrible," I finish for him.

"Awful." He throws his arms up.

We start cracking up so hard I stop and brace myself with my crutches so I don't fall over. When I get enough control over my breathing, I squeak out through waves of laughter, "They were just talking heads up there."

Jason clutches his stomach and says between snorts, "No characters…no movement…I think they were trying to get by on witty banter?"

"But they forgot the witty part."

"It just went nowhere." He starts imitating the mumbliest actor with his hands in his pockets, throwing out big words that don't have a point.

I stiffen and make robot noises, "Boo-bee-bop-boop," because that's what they sounded like to me. After going back and forth with our mumbler and robot impressions, we lose it in another fit.

When the second fit fades, I start crutching back toward our dorms. "Are we being too mean? Were our expectations too high?"

"Probably. But we've also seen a lot of improv, so we know. And I know that right now I don't want to be part of that group."

"Maybe they had an off night," I offer.

"Maybe."

I stop on a little bridge over a pond to watch the moonlight reflecting on the water. "Maybe we start our own group."

Jason puts his hands gently on my shoulders and kisses the nape of my neck. "Definitely."

"We could incorporate video into our form somehow, like you were talking about."

"I love that idea. Your brain is my favorite," he says, getting back to kissing my neck and making my limbs so weak I'm close to losing my grip on the crutch handles.

My voice gets crackly as I try to persist with my inspiration. "We could name our group The Harrietts," I say, thinking of my new pet goldfish. Harriett is smaller and spottier than Harold, but just as helpful. I promised her we'd all have great adventures together—though Harriett's will be strictly from the safety of her bowl.

I turn to face Jason, and he lifts me onto the broad rail of the bridge. "Yes, let's," he says, as my crutches clatter to the ground.

Acknowledgments

I've been working on this book in one version or another for over a decade, and I would not be writing this without the help and support of everyone included here.

I'm grateful to my phenomenal and dedicated editor, Candace Havens. Thank you for believing in this story, for pushing me to make it better, and for your humor and kindness along the way. (Insert all the deleted exclamation points here.) To the entire powerhouse team at Entangled: thank you for putting your creativity, savvy, and heart into this book, and for all your behind-the-scenes magic. I love being part of this visionary house.

I'm grateful to my agent, Leon Husock. Thanks, too, to the other writers Leon represents who welcomed me into their secret hangout.

Thank you to author Tamora Pierce. You've given me many gifts, the greatest being your example of what it is to be a young adult writer and the inspiration to become one myself.

Thank you to everyone at Lighthouse Writers Workshop

in Denver, particularly: Andrea Dupree and Mike Henry for cultivating this community; Lisa Jensen for introducing me to Lighthouse; Shana Kelly for your edits early on and your publishing advice when I needed it; and to all the students who took workshops with me. Also, big thanks to Sarah Ockler, for your guidance as my first young adult writing teacher and for being excited to read the final version.

To Victoria Hanley: I'm so lucky I signed up for your young adult writing workshop all those years ago, and the one after that, and the one after that… Thank you a million times over for everything you've taught me, for your masterful editing, and most of all, for giving me faith in my writing and being my champion.

Enormous thanks to my superstar critique partners, who are also my good friends. To Maura Weiler: for your always-insightful edits and suggestions and for leading the way as the first published author of our group. You are a badass. To Susan Knudten: for your faith, spot-on edits, willingness to wordsmith something (well and quickly) at every stage of this process, and for being there time and again to celebrate the good news and pull me through the disappointments. Also, for all the laughs and wigs with The Novelistas. Big love.

Many thanks to my dear friends who read early versions of this manuscript and whose influences still live in the pages: Kate McFee, Megan Martin, Pam Farone, and Tricia McKinnon.

To my friends, neighbors, and extended family who have cheered me on: thank you, and I love you. A special shout-out goes to Shannon McDaniel for the many chats during the rollercoaster to publication. Thanks also to Sarah Gilbert and everyone at RHR International for your flexibility and encouragement.

I turned to my Facebook friends to brainstorm a few changes. To Chris Stock: thank you for the sketch inspiration and for making me feel like I already had a fan. Thank you to Jaime Hara Koch for suggesting Scared Scriptless and to Doug Reuter for giving me a cheesy cancer joke. How awesome is crowdsourcing writing? Thanks to all who offered suggestions.

To everyone I've performed with over the years: thank you for the laughs and bits that have fueled me. Especially, and with bear hugs, to my first improv family: Andy MacDonald, Ben Reed, Brian McManus, Matt Love, Perry Daniel, and Tim Vierling, You gave me a way of life and inspiration for this book.

Thank you to Judy, Rhonda, Tim, and the entire big, beautiful clan that I was lucky enough to marry into. I'm grateful for your support now and for how you were there for me like family even before it was official.

All my love and gratitude goes to my immediate family. To Don Alan, thank you for being a way better dad than the one in this book, for giving me the gift of curiosity, and for teaching me to always keep reading and learning. To my mom, Evelyn Alan, thank you for your fierce love and unshakeable faith in me, for teaching me grit and perseverance, and for always, always being there for me. To my sister, Theresa Alan, my earliest champion in life and in art. It is so helpful to have a bestselling author in the family, especially one that shares the same sense of humor. I'm grateful for your infinite guidance, all the edits, and for teaching me that the upside of tragedy is that it can be transformed into art.

To Emerson, my mighty and amazing daughter. Thank you for making my heart grow bigger. To Brian, my witness in life. Thank you for inspiring the words in Craig and Jason's song from your poetry to me, for your boundless support in every way possible, and for this messy, beautiful life we've created together.

Author's Note

While this story is Ellie's, it is inspired by my own journey with chondrosarcoma. I was in my twenties when I was diagnosed, and my path to recovery included fewer disco balls and many more visits with surgeons. The people who helped me through that time in my life made it possible for me to write this book, and I would be remiss not to mention them here.

I'm eternally grateful to my miracle surgeon, John Healey (could there be a better name for a doctor?), and everyone at Memorial Sloan Kettering Cancer Center who cared for me.

Thank you to Kim and John Smith for the gift of a consultation with Stritter Medical Consulting, and to Gwendolyn Stritter for working with me pro bono and guiding me through finding treatment for a rare cancer. I wish our healthcare system was such that everyone could have a medical advisor when they needed one.

Thank you to Mary Sorens of ABC Survivors and Bruce and Beverly of the Liddy Shriver Sarcoma Initiative. Thank you to Elizabeth Moonrose of the Chondrosarcoma Support Care Community for answering my questions as a patient back then and later as a writer researching the realities of a teen chondrosarcoma diagnosis. Any inaccuracies that remain are mine alone. On behalf of the community, thank you for your enduring compassion and contribution.

Thank you to Peter and Deb Thomas for opening up your home to me, a generosity that still moves me today. Thank you to Yolanda Cruz for your steady kindness. I'm grateful to the entire McManus family for your support of every kind through it all. To Marian and Dick Bott: thank you for making it possible to get to Germany and back for a fifth opinion and for welcoming me in, giving me a home, and making sure I was cared for in New York. It was everything. Thank you to Jen Nails, Mignon Remé, Patricia Beck, Frau Strauss, and again to Susan (before we were even bosom friends), for offering support, connections, and places to stay in Düsseldorf and Münster. And to Bill Capron and Lizabeth Gottsegen for your healing magic. You all forever cemented my knowing that the world is more good and kind than not.

To Team Brunch—Brian, Matt, Megan, Perry, and Tim: thank you for being by my side through it all, for holding me up, and for figuratively and literally catching me before I fell. And again to my mom: for taking a month off to care for me. I'm grateful we made it to the other side, together.

Thank you to everyone who sent me prayers and good vibes. I felt the full power of your healing thoughts. There are many more people who helped me who I have not named (hard to imagine, but true), and I'm grateful to you all. Finally, to everyone who has faced cancer or cared for someone with it, my love goes out to you.

About the Author

Sara Jade Alan wrote her first comedy sketch during second-grade recess, then cast it, directed it, and made costumes out of garbage bags. Since then, she has performed in over a thousand improvised and scripted shows all over the country. Currently she is one-half of the comedy duo, The Novelistas, who perform about writing and teach performance to writers. Originally from a suburb of Chicago, Sara now lives in Colorado with her husband and daughter.

Discover more Entangled Teen books...

FALLING FOR FOREVER
a *Before Forever* novel by Melissa Chambers

If Jenna wants to make it to L.A. to extend her fifteen minutes of reality-show fame, she'll need to win her high school's talent competition. Standing in her way is Miles Cleveland, the music nerd with a stick up his butt and a bone to pick with Jenna herself. Miles has his own reasons for needing to win, and he can't question his plan, no matter how deep Jenna buries into his heart.

DIARY OF A TEENAGE JEWEL THIEF
a novel by Rosie Somers

Most sixteen-year-olds shouldn't know where museums keep their rarest jewels (the basement) but for Marisol Flores, a life of jewel thievery is a birthright handed down, even if she didn't ask for it. So when a rival thief targets Mari and her mother, Mari's more than happy to flee to bustling New York City. Blending in is a dream come true but keeping her secret gets way more complicated when handsome Will Campbell sets his sights on her. She can't help but like his terrible puns and charming grin but when her past catches up with her, it's not only her life at stake. Will could be next.

OTHER BREAKABLE THINGS
a novel by Kelley York and Rowan Altwood

According to Japanese legend, folding a thousand paper cranes will grant you healing. Evelyn Abel will fold two thousand if it will bring Luc back to her. After a car crash got Luc Argent a second chance at life, he tried to embrace it. But he always knew death could be right around the corner again. And now it is. A road trip to Oregon—where death with dignity is legal—is his answer. But along for the ride is his best friend, Evelyn. And she's not giving up so easily.

CPSIA information can be obtained
at www.ICGtesting.com
Printed in the USA
FSHW02n0718180518
48402FS